℘FLUFF℘

A MODERN DECAMERON OF LUST AND LICENTIOUSNESS

by

CHARLES NUETZEL

The Borgo Press
An Imprint of Wildside Press

MMVII

FIRST EDITION

⚘CONTENTS⚘

℘INTRODUCTION℘

A word of advice. This collection is called *Fluff* for a very good reason, which will become clear enough after a while. There is nothing really at all serious here, just short things that got published for one reason or another a couple or three decades ago. They are illustrative of the so-called "adult" publications of the mid-twentieth century.

This is a collection of light seductions published in what was in the 1960s considered girlie magazines. These periodicals ran a lot of pictures of partly nude (from the waist up, natch) ladies of breasty development, framing stories of equally revealing subject matter. The editorial requirements were tales of around 3,000 words that involved at least one lady being shown as bare as possible and then ravished in some way or another, to the delight of the hero of the story. In some cases there were short articles, serious or otherwise. But this was the pulp field for beginning writers or full-time professionals knocking out pages filled with swiftly typed copy.

And Alex Blake, John Davidson, Stu Rivers, Lex Lexington, C. A. Ning, Alexis Charles, are just a few of the pen names offered up as bylines to confuse and confound the massive audience who generally ignored the words in favor of the lovely visions of half-naked vamps of rather voluptuous development that stared out from every page in seductive invitation.

This is where I began my writing career. I offer these stories as an example of the times, and hopefully some very light and *fluffy* reading for the reader. Most were written during my first year as a writer, for later, once I sold my first paperback novel, I discovered that longer stories were more ideally suited to my rather wordy style. I wrote very little short fiction after that, much of which is now being offered as a separate book by Wildside Press (*Dimensions*).

It was a grand way to learn how to write and at the same time getting paid hard cash for my efforts.

Here we supply a number of such stories, many of them merely pure seductive fluff, plus a few with a bit more meat to them. I promise little more than a momentary escape into the fantasyland of seductive females being chased after by desperate young men out to discover the thrills they can share together.

Ah, the magic of it all.

But, nevertheless, pure fluff.

—CHARLES NUETZEL
THOUSAND OAKS, CALIFORNIA
August 2006

ಹFITTE THE FIRSTಜ

Talk about fluff. This is prime fluff, and a good starting place, I suppose. From here the fluff gets less fluffy in some cases and somewhat crazy fluffy in others. But this one! I probably typed a title and then simply began writing. Well, just don't expect too much! We'll call this simply a Teaser! And this lady just teased her hubby to distraction. Rather a mean thing to do, under the circumstances. But you couldn't blame him, nor could you blame her.

*DON'T CRY TONIGHT*ಜ

The way June taunted him was disgusting. Posing nude before the mirror, striking positions that accented the lovely curves and swells of the body.

"Don't you think I'm darling?" she cooed, looking across at him in the reflection. "Jimmy...don't you think I'm the sexiest thing you ever did see?"

A mad knot choked his throat. He tried to swallow it down. The lump bounced back into place. It was a hard, heated thing that made his heart beat faster and faster.

"You sexy bitch!" he cursed, standing and stepping toward her. "I'll have you for that!" He grabbed at her and she easily dipped under his awkward arms.

"Jimmy can't get me, he can't get me!" she teased laughingly, a nasty snarl twisting her features.

The blood was pounding in his veins. Just the sight of her luscious body, with its bouncing breasts, and grinding hips, sent stabs of desire flooding across him like a hot wave

7

of nausea.

"You dirty bitch!" he screeched, lunging again for her. This time his fingers made contact, and he squeezed them tightly around her arm. Viciously he pulled her toward him. She struggled with him, violently.

"Let go, Jim...please...you'll mess me all up for to-night..." She twisted and turned in his arms, trying to get away from his passionate embrace. His lips were hungrily attempting to make contact with hers.

"Please!" she pleaded in a high-pitched, almost sick-sounding voice. Then his mouth clamped over hers for a long and penetrating kiss. With all her strength she pushed against his chest. He felt the angry dig of her long nails as they clawed at him. "Let go...you brute!"

"Christ!" he cursed, stepping away in fury. "What's wrong with a man having a little with his wife? What's wrong with that?"

She had turned to the mirror and her eyes were already taking that cold icy gaze she always gave him when he began talking about sex to her. The first few months of their marriage had been all fire and passion, now it had cooled off, and he didn't like it.

Her hands cupped under her breasts, lifting them upwards, forcing the nipples forward and rigidly tight and tempting.

She turned to look at him again. "I don't know what's gotten into you, Jimmy...all you want is to have it over and over...after all, how much can a girl take?" As she spoke her fingers were thoughtfully caressing the erect pink dots that seemed to be, of their own free will, asking for him. But he knew what she was doing. She taunted him every night before she went to work. She teased and showed off her body to him, posing and pinching the right places so that the desire would shake through him. She was a devil. She liked to make him nervously hot throughout his body, it seemed to give her some kind of thrill or kick.

Suddenly he was mad, furious clean through. She didn't have to do what she did. Nobody could take what she handed out!

For the first time in months he didn't care what she

thought, or what she did afterwards. He would have her!

Tonight!

"You haven't given out to me for over a month...what kind of person do you think I am? I gotta...gotta have you..." As he stepped toward her his breath was getting heavy, and every nerve was fiery with the desire to kiss her, caress those lovely, youthful orbs of flesh which she was still fingering at the mirror.

"You do think I'm sexy, don't you?" she asked again, not aware that he was so close, or the determined frame of his mind.

"You're the sexiest...and you're giving out to your husband tonight!" he snapped, lunging up to her and caressing her smooth white arms. She murmured delightfully. She liked that, he knew. She loved to be fondled and caressed, just like a cat. He would fondle and caress her tonight. She wasn't going out to work, she'd give out to him tonight, the little whoring bitch!

"You do have a nice touch, Jim..." she sighed looking up at him. The light in her eyes was a little softer for a moment. But only a moment. The coldness returned. "No, you can't have me...not tonight...maybe not ever!"

His hands clamped tighter on her shoulders. Then he swung her bodily around. He forced his mouth to hers, ramming his tongue searchingly for hers. She struggled, like always. But when one of his hands cupped up under her breasts he could feel that it was warm. He caressed her gently, then more forcefully. A moan sighed out of her and he knew he was on first base. She struggled desperately, but it was a losing battle. She was a real sexed woman, and once the right buttons had been pushed she wouldn't stop—she couldn't!

There wouldn't be any work for her tonight!

But he didn't care. So they didn't get the extra money...he wanted her to stop anyway. But she said he couldn't help her enough.

Yes, now she was going, her hips pushing up against his, her lips parting like wild, and her tongue moving frantically with his.

Tonight she was his!

FLUFF, BY CHARLES NUETZEL

* * * * * * *

The next day when she reported for work she was bawled out cruelly.

"You know we needed you...a lot of men were asking for you...and when you don't show up, it's bad for business..."

"I'm sorry, but my husband all but...well, raped me! With all the work we have had the last months I've just not been able to have the energy for him...and anyway I don't like him that way as much since working here. After all experience shows a girl something," she laughed, as the other woman started walking out of the room. "And, after all, he got me started on this racket...he has only himself to blame! But last night...I just couldn't stop him..."

"Well, don't let it happen again...if he wants you to work nights, he can pay just like the customers, waiting his turn...just because he paid a few bucks for a marriage..."

"I'm sorry," she said, arranging her nude body so that it would show off the best lines of her sex-appeal for the man now waiting outside in the hall. "Let the man in..." she announced, smiling her lips professionally so that he would be feeling at ease...

She could hardly wait! She thought as the customer started undressing.

He looks so strong!

*I bet he'll be a good one...*she sighed as he slip down beside her. Then as their bodies made the first contact she knew he would be good.

Oh God! Better than Jimmy-boy, so much better!

10

১০FITTE THE SECOND০৪

Hollywood as an industry is a sneaky business with as many curves as a lovely lady in heat. Everybody is seeking a way to make a move up in the climb to fame. Sometimes the play gets an unexpected payoff. Of course, sometimes a downer can be an upper. Or in this case, it could be sideways. Showbiz lifts its hungry head in this bit of...

*PARTY BUSINESS*০৪

"Say, you're new here, aren't you?" the woman asked, eyes fairly raking over his body. All he noticed was that this female was nicely attractive; but just one of countless wannabe actresses, or mere party girls that decorated such affairs. How could he know she would turn out to be special?

Dan Carnes didn't know what he was doing at the Belfort party. It was Belfort who had kept him from getting a role in that picture the man was producing. Big Name Star Johnny Belfort.

But Carnes' agent had told him to get to that party and "ride with the punches!" and they would see what tomorrow brought in way of a part.

Well, as far as Dan was concerned you could take these so-called Hollywood blow-outs and shove them! He'd been to several. Women presented themselves in the best tradition of the silver screen. Low-cut, bulging breast-lines. Bleach blonde hair—unless they'd had blonde hair to begin with, and then it was red or black—tight fitting dresses created by one or another top Hollywood fashion designer and borrowed from every studio costume department. But these were the "look, but don't touch" variety of women—except for some high class producer or director. That was the trouble; a woman had an edge when it came to getting parts in movies, and if she was the type that normally ran around, she had it made.

But that was the least of Dan's troubles. His problem was on two levels. One was frustration that no matter what he did, things seemed to end up exactly like before: failure! The other problem was connected to that: financial. He had needed that part in the Johnny Belfort new movie. And there had been no reason to be turned down. Just like all the other times, a person needed more than talent, good looks and a winning personality. You had to know someone. Without that important contact you had to take the time developing one. Like going to parties. Hollywood parties where everybody stood around listening to the jokes of the big boys; laughing—even if nothing was funny...and trying to get an edge on all the other slobs who were out to beat you in the eyes of the important people.

So, around and around it all went.

"Say...you're new here, aren't you?" she said again. He nodded and tried to keep his eyes away from the lovely crevice between her large, creamy breasts which was almost completely revealed because of the low cut of the dress top.

"With anybody?" she asked, stepping forward. It was one of those slinky movements of her body which seemed to push her exciting round hips forward.

"I...well..." was all that he could manage.

"I'm all alone, too...in a way." She made a sidelong glance toward a group of people who were crowding around the Big Star. "Mind keeping me company?"

That was one thing he wouldn't mind. If there was anything which would help to cut the bitter taste of defeat from his throat, it would be a sexy young woman like this one. He let her take his arm and lead him through the room. A moment later he was surprised to find that they had stepped out onto the patio. The lighting was dim and he could hear the music of the three-piece combo playing in the background.

For a long moment they stood in the semi-darkness, just

12

looking at each other. Then she half turned away from him, her face seeming to shade slightly pink. "You have the remarkable stare," she told him in a throaty way.

"I'm sorry about that."

"Don't be. I liked it." She turned toward him again, and then, taking hold of his hand, led him to a small table which had two patio chairs by it.

"You seem to know your way around here pretty well," he pointed out, sitting and idly working the glass of scotch in his hands. He found it hard to look in her direction. She was far too beautiful and desirable. Naturally he'd leap in bed with her the moment she made any subtle hint that this was what she was after. But, for the moment, he had to wait, and the waiting was all the more difficult when he looked at that flowing, well built figure.

She laughed. "I've been around here quite a long while."

"How's that?"

"Let's not ask questions about ourselves. Just enjoy the evening. The night. The dim lights and music. The cocktails. Each other. Make believe that we have known each other for a long time...that we are at the annual country dance. Maybe we're sweethearts or lovers or married..."

He felt his insides dig slightly. There were mixed emotions rushing through him. What kind of nut had he run into this time? If he didn't know Hollywood, he might say it was the town. But the fact was that everybody who seriously wanted to build a career was too busy building it to be "nutty"; regardless of popular belief, it was far from a crazy industry. It was cold business spiced with big egos and big business money. There were nuts, all right. But.

"Don't you think this is sorta fast?" he asked, taking a swallow of his drink.

"Hardly."

"We don't even know each other's names." He tried to smile.

"Oh, that's not hard. You're Dan Carnes and I thought you knew who I was. I'm Mrs. Johnny Belfort. But you can call me Karen."

That one made him gulp several other swallows of his scotch.

"What the hell?" was all that he could say.

"Oh, it's quite simple. I saw you in Johnny's office the other day. You were too concerned with...well, other things. I know how it is with young struggling actors. And ..."

"I don't get it!"

"I wanted to meet you. It was simple to just call your agent."

That explained a lot. Why he had been brought to this party so quickly. One moment he hadn't known anything about it, and then the next he'd been given the good old push.

Which had landed him right in the lap of Mrs. Johnny Belfort. That would help a lot. He was suddenly mad at his agent. And a little mad at this woman. And a lot mad at himself.

But there wasn't anything that he could do about it now. Except get out of the situation as gracefully as possible.

He stood, looking at his watch. "Oh, my God!" he exclaimed, in a voice which sounded even faked in his own ears.

"Sit down, and stop acting silly!" Karen Belfort told him in a stern voice. "Stop acting silly!"

He was surprised by the harsh quality of her words. So shocked that he did as she told him.

"You don't think that this is just a casual pass, do you?"

She leaned across the table, looking at him for a long time. "I don't make casual passes!"

Her mood changed then. She smiled. Leaned back and then drank from the glass in her hands. "I liked the looks of you the moment I saw you in hubby's office..." Her voice drifted off.

"I'm afraid that I don't understand," he told her, downing the rest of his drink.

"Let's not worry about that." She looked directly into his eyes. "Let's talk about other things..."

She stood and taking hold of his hand, pulled him after her. They walked through the living room, which was filled with scores of important Hollywood personalities.

She ignored them. A moment later they were walking up a staircase.

"You don't mind telling me what..."

She turned sparkling eyes in his direction as they entered a long hallway. "My, my, you are innocent, aren't you?" she smiled, squeezing his hand.

He didn't want to think about what must be going through her mind. He was just numb, only following her because he couldn't think of anything else to do. In a few moments they were in a large bedroom, the door closed and locked.

She turned and slid both arms around his neck. He felt the soft pressure of her body as it blended against his. Her lips caressed his mouth.

He just stood there, too numb to respond. Things were not only happening too fast, they were a little blunt and brazen.

"What's wrong?" she demanded. "Don't you like girls?" She looked deep into his eyes. "Or is it just me?"

He gulped nervously, dropping his eyes to the floor. "Let's just say that I don't go for shacking up with somebody's wife."

She laughed. Her lovely head fell backwards and her lips opened wide; and she laughed.

"You're kidding. You must be!" She backed away. Then her hands went in back of her and a moment later the dress slid to the floor. She'd been wearing nothing else underneath.

He just gaped at her.

She was just about the loveliest woman he had ever seen. Her breasts large, but rigid and firm. Her waist narrow and slender, spreading out into curving hips and tapering down to full, solid thighs and legs.

"Don't be a silly child." She told him, stepping up close and then pressing against his body. "I want you. That's all that should matter!"

"Don't...don't you think that this is rather sudden?"

A giggle bubbled up through her chest and out past her lips. "I don't see where you get your square ideas. This is Hollywood! Live, love and have a ball!" She wiggled against him. When he didn't respond she stepped back a little. "Look, if you're really serious about...about worrying...just

15

see it my way. Johnny-boy is a big star. Girls fall all over him. And he uses their bodies each and every time he can. He plays around. So, I play around."

"But why? When he has somebody like you?" Dan gulped, beginning to break down his resistance. His arms were already sliding around her back.

"You know how it is. A woman in hand never is like the one across the street."

Their lips met passionately. He responded with every ounce of physical energy he had in him.

"See what I mean?" she told him, leading him toward the bed. "Just like the new lover is always better than the old one!"

He slid down next to her a few moments later, and for a long time they locked in a series of meaningful embraces. "You won't regret this," she sighed, breathless. "Believe me, you won't regret it ..."

After that neither of them were saying anything. And just before he floated down through the pit of burning, fiery passion, one thought flashed though his mind: it was a gas on Big Shot Actor, Johnny Belfort...the man had turned him down for a movie role, but his wife hired him for a lovers' role.

It wasn't until the next morning, when his agent called, that he realized the price that Mrs. Karen Belfort had been willing to pay for the service he had rendered the evening before, or exactly what she had meant when she'd told him that he wouldn't regret making love to her. As if he could ever regret making love to any woman as beautiful as she was.

The voice was excited and loud in his ears, as his agent told him the news, "Its just like I figured ... and have told you—there is always more than one way to make a powerful friend in Hollywood. Apparently you came through with flying colors. Johnny Belfort called and said that he decided that you would be perfect for the role...wives do have influence..."

The rest he didn't hear. After the phone had been hung up, it rang again.

This time it was Karen Belfort. He didn't have to guess

16

what she would want. He had a few more installments to make for her help in getting him his first big break in movies.

And he was determined to pay, in full!

ഔFITTE THE THIRDᏒ

In Hollywood there are all kinds of jobs. Some work; some don't. Some are a dead end, some are chances to get ahead in this land of film making. Some people will go to any means to survive and get a great film part. Some times it actually works. Consider this situation and maybe you'll understand what we're talking about.

*THE STAND-IN*Ꮢ

It was like a scene from a Ben Taylor movie, except that the director didn't say "cut" when things were just getting interesting.

The girl's name was Gloria—at this point the last name wasn't of any importance. The only important fact was that she was bare from the waist up, and her full womanly charms were holding the complete attention of the man's fascinated gaze.

"You're quite lovely, my dear," he told her in that voice which is so famous on the silver screen. "So very lovely."

"Oh, I'm glad you like me, and all that!" Gloria announced, wiggling herself closer to him. The action caused her curving supple breasts to swing and bob. "Do you think I have the shape for that Miss Simpson role you called me up here to interview for?"

"Well, now, my dear, you have to understand that this will all depend on..."

Her lips cut him off with a kiss. "Is that what you're talking about?" she asked, moving away.

18

He grabbed for her, but she managed to keep her distance.

"Such a lovely lady," he said, his eyes paralyzed by the inviting womanhood of her body.

"Then I get the part?" her eyes were eager and her lips smiling happily.

"Well...now, I don't know!"

The dress dropped lower as the young girl stood. "You mean that if I do certain favors for you...I get the part?" she asked, stepping over the circle of her dress which was in a ring on the floor.

The man coughed, nervously.

It was like a scene from a Ben Taylor movie, except that the director didn't say "cut" when things were just getting interesting.

"Well, you might say that would certainly help matters."

She moved up to him. Pressing her breasts against his chest. Her lips brushed his.

"Say you'll give me the part, if I go to bed with you," she murmured in a throaty voice.

"Well...now, that all..."

Her lips caressed his for a moment and then they parted in a deep passion kiss.

"Say you'll give me the part," she pleaded in his ear, half breathless in her own passion. "Tell me...just tell me."

He shrugged, pulling her closer.

"Of course, my dear."

"Tell me...in words. Say it out!"

"Okay,' he laughed, lifting her in his arms and carrying her across the room toward a low, large lounge. "If you let me make love to you, I'll give you a part in the movie!"

In the next morning mail there was a type plain brown envelop, with simple type-written name and address of Ben Taylor. It was with the other morning mail. He hardly noticed it at first. It was saved until last and even then he almost didn't open it.

In the side were two photo-proofs which showed the world-wise famous Ben Taylor as he had never been seen on the screen. He was stretched out on a large lounge, locked in a wild embrace with a delightfully youthful female. Gloria!

19

It didn't leave anything to his imagination.

A note was attached. It simply read: "If you don't want this to go to the press, along with a complete tape recording of the whole thing that went on last night, then I'd advise you to meet me at..."

The rest was a Beverly Hills address and the time given was that very day at three-thirty.

He just smiled. Almost tauntingly and walked over to his phone and dialed the studio.

"Hello, Henry?" he said to his producer. "Yeah, it's me, Ben right. I wonder if you could do me a favor? Thanks. You know my stand-in. Could you have him meet me at my apartment? Right, my place in Hollywood."

He smiled once more, as he hung up the phone.

* * * * * * *

His stand-in sat quietly as Ben outlined the whole thing. "You see, they are trying to blackmail me and they could easily get away with it—except for you..."

The man just smiled after Taylor was finished. He could have been the famous actor's twin brother. The sound of voice, the looks, and actions were perfected down to the last detail.

"You *see,* with your help," Taylor told his double, "they will never be able to prove it was me. All any lawyer would have to say is that it was you...not me! And who will prove differently?"

For the first time since he had arrived at the actor's apartment, the stand-in spoke.

"But you don't understand..."

"What don't I understand?"

"Well, tell me, have you ever been in the place that I am, now?"

"What do you mean?"

"Just that, well, as an actor I'm finished. I don't have a chance, unless I had my face changed. Because you are so famous, nobody will give me a part except as your double."

Taylor looked at the man for a long time. "Oh, I think I see what you mean..." He thought for a moment and then continued, "I meant to mention that there would be a lot of money in it for you...enough to get your face changed—if that's what you want."

The other man just smiled in that famous way that Taylor had made immortal. "But I don't think you understand." He paused for a moment and then looked directly into Taylor's eyes. "It's a very good offer...but you see, I want more! Much more."

"What?"

"Let's say...half of your salary?"

The great man gulped. "That's probably more than the people want who are blackmailing me!"

"No it isn't!" That smile projected itself on Taylor's double, once more. "Because, like I said; you don't understand! I'm the blackmailer!"

‌FITTE THE FOURTH‌

Okay, I'll admit it, right from the start, this is one of those stories that happened as a necessity of grinding out material for publication in mags of questionable reputation. So...here we have a fella who is about to climb into bed with his brother's future wife. Another bit of rather raw fluff!

A REPUTATION AT STAKE‌

He could hardly believe it. What was he doing in Nora Jenson's apartment?

He was a married man.

And she was the girlfriend of his brother; in fact she was the girl his brother planned to marry.

So what was he doing, sitting on her sofa, sipping a drink, and waiting while she was changing into something more comfortable?

It still seemed more like a dream than reality.

A man just didn't start making passes at his future sister-in-law.

Or did he?

Here he was, not only ready-willing-and-able, but waiting for the fireworks to begin.

Nora Jenson, a beautiful blonde, with wide, innocent eyes.

A doll, hot, bothered, and about ready to prove that all her curving bulges and dipping valleys were really hers. And why?

Because Brother Jim had asked that they get together.

He still found it hard to believe that any man would be willing to let another, especially his own brother, sleep with the girl he was in love with. And about to marry.

But then Jim was an odd one.

So was Nora, too.

An odd pair, to say the least!

They made a cool couple. A wild twosome. A nutty relationship if he had ever seen one.

Just the night before, Jim had come to his home, asked that the two of them go out alone for a ride, and then once alone in the car he popped up with his request.

"Carl," Jim said, guiding the car onto the freeway. "I want you to take Nora Jenson out tomorrow night."

"You what?"

"Take my girl out...and seduce her!"

"Take her out and seduce her?" Carl gulped nervously, unable to believe his ears. "You crazy, Jim? You plain crazy?"

"No, not at all!"

Then he had gone on to explain. He had his reputation at stake.

"Hell, I have my personal happiness at stake!" Carl cried. "What about my wife? If she found out, that would be the end!"

"But this is important. Nora is a doll, hottest woman I ever knew, a real whammie in the bed chamber...you'll like her. I know you'll be crazy about the way she makes with the necking and petting and hot lips; she's really the end."

"You're daft! What's gotten into you?"

"What's gotten into *you*? A couple of years back, before you get married to Terry, you would have jumped at the chance of getting the gifts of a lovely woman like Nora. Believe me you'll never regret it. Believe me!"

He still couldn't believe what was happening.

Here he was, in Nora Jenson's apartment.

The bedroom door opened, and in walked the most beautiful female creature he had ever seen.

She was sure a doll. Brother Jim surely could pick them! Real winners.

What hips! Rolling, swaying. What a *flat,* smooth stomach!

Wonderful balls of chest material. Bouncing. Bobbing. Pink-tipped.

Her hips seemed to be doing an extra amount of swaying.

He liked that!

"Hi, baby!" she said, sliding down into his arms.

When he caressed her nude breasts she moaned.

When he kissed her lips she signed and shivered.

When their tongues met, a convulsive tremor ran through her.

"Man, what happened?" she exclaimed excitedly, looking up at him. "This is the best!"

Then they stopped talking and got down to the real business of seduction.

She never knew the truth. And what was that?

Part of it was that her husband-to-be was out with another woman that night, doing much the same as they were doing. In fact he was out with Carl's wife, Terry—though Carl knew nothing of this, of course!

Another part dealt with other information...like the fact that Jim had some reputation with the ladies, and he had made a boast with several friends that he could seduce any woman in the world, if given enough time.

Being a man of honor, he was stuck with his promise when his friends who had challenged his statement (or brag) suggesting that he couldn't seduce his sister-in-law

Well, what could a guy do? He did it. It was simple.

Terry never knew the truth, any more than Nora did.

For how would the two women in question be expected to tell identical twins apart, during only one a night-session?

They might wonder at the difference...but they never knew.

৪০FITTE THE FIFTH৫ও

And here we continue in the kingdom of Filmland. This came from a conversation I had with a woman who was in show-business. She told me how during an interview she was approached in this manner, though in her case she was sophisticated enough to simply side-step the man's demands. This is merely a fictional extension, based on: what if she had played along? So here's a bit of fluff about that...

*COUCH INTERVIEW*৫ও

Norma Fosse didn't know whether to be nervous, scared or excited. This was her first real interview with a live-wire assistant director. It could mean her big break! And she had prepared herself the best way she knew how. A low cut, slinky red dress which showed every lovely curve of her youthful form. One thing she did know was, she had an outstanding figure. Her breasts were well formed and full; and most important they were firm. Such a dress as she had on now was made for her.

But still she was partly scared. It had something to do with what her roommate had told her just before she left.

"Norma...just remember, forget that country attitude of yours."

"What do you mean by that?" she had asked, feeling a crimson flush of anger warm her cheeks.

"Just that...well, you know!" Her roommate had hesitated for moment, seeming to find difficulty choosing the right words. "Well, you know. Play along with him."

An icy flutter had chilled through her. "I don't know…"

"Look, Norma. If you want to get ahead, you just can't have those closed moral ideas you have."

"But how would I know I'd get the part after I'd…I'd done that?" She bit her lip at thought of what the other girl was suggesting.

"You don't. But believe me, you won't have any chance if you…well, don't play up to him!"

And playing up to him meant doing anything he asked. Not that she hadn't been to bed with a man before, but she didn't believe that a woman should let a man make love to her unless there was some honest emotion involve.

Nervously she walked into the outer office of Walter Bayles' business offices.

The secretary looked up, impersonally. Her lips smiled, but she was all professional business.

"I'm Miss Fosse," Norma announced, stepping up to the other woman's desk. "Mr. Bayles is expecting me."

The secretary nodded. "Have a seat, I'll tell him you're here."

Then the waiting. There must have been twenty minutes of agonizing waiting.

Finally a voice sounded from the small box on the secretary's desk. "You can tell Miss Fosse to come in, now."

The cold knot of fear choked through her chest and throat. Swallowing hard, then taking several deep breaths, she stood and walked through the door which the secretary indicated with a nod and smile.

The door closed behind her and she felt suddenly like a trapped animal. There wasn't any turning back, now. Everything which she did would mean something in the gaze of the large, squat man who was eagerly eyeing the curving swell of her v-neckline.

He stood and smiled. It was one of those professional muscle movements of his lips which are so famous in Hollywood.

"Have a seat, Miss Fosse." His arm dramatically indicated a chair across the desk from his large swivel chair. "I must say that you are by far lovelier than your agent, Mr. Landers, said."

She felt a shiver of revulsion move through her. The thought of playing along with him made her feel sick inside.

"I understand you are interested in the Denton part."

She just nodded, gripping her purse tightly with her hands.

Suddenly she was wondering why Hollywood had been so glamorous sounding in Henderson's Creek. Maybe just because she'd been anxious to get out of that hick-water town where she had been born, raised and lived all her life. But right now, faced with her first real challenge, she felt like a fool.

"Have you ever had any acting experience?" he asked, finding it hard to keep his eyes away from where the tight fitting dress met the cream-smooth whiteness of her breasts.

"Didn't Mr. Landers tell you all that?" she asked, her voice having an edge of frantic nervousness to it.

"Well, he did say something...I don't really remember. You know agents. One ear and out the other. All they do is yak-yak all the time. Even if you took the time to listen, you couldn't believe what they're saying."

She couldn't help smiling at that. For a moment she almost found it possible to relax. He wasn't really as bad as she had built him up in her mind. The man was leaning back in his chair, just looking her over; but all men will look a beautiful woman over a bit—it's just normal. In fact, it was actually flattering; it proved that there might even be some real logic to her wanting to get into movies.

"You know, Miss Fosse, this part isn't really much, Just a walk in and out. No lines."

She nodded, smiled, trying to make it pleasant looking. "I realize that, Mr. Bayles. But a girl has to start some place." That was a slip and she felt a flutter of fear shoot through her. One thing that Mr. Landers had told her sometime ago: *you have to lie through your teeth!*

"What I mean, is..." she began to explain, "start with you, of course."

He laughed, almost pleasantly. Don't explain. I like your honesty."

"But...I really..."

"Don't. Anybody can see that you're scared to death.

27

This is your first interview, isn't it?"

She just nodded. She was looking down at the purse in her hands. Her lower lip hurt where she'd been lightly biting it.

"Don't be worried. Everybody is nervous on their first interview. It's just normal."

He stood and stepped around his desk. A moment later he was standing over her. He looked down. From his point-of-view she knew he could probably see down her neck clear to the navel. Her first impulse was to shift her position, and she half started. Then she remembered that it was better to play along—and anyway there wasn't a thing wrong with letting him have a free thrill. Let him peek all he wants!

"You are a lovely woman," he told her, reaching for one of her hands. He folded his beefy thick fingers around hers. "So delicate and nice."

His voice was lower and deeper, the words more full sounding. "Stand up for me!"

She stood, not knowing what to expect. For a moment she was terrified that he would make a pass but instead he dropped her hand.

"Turn around."

She turned.

"Yes, yes. You are quite a lovely woman. I don't know if you're quite right for the Denton part. She's just a maid, but...maybe..." His voice became slightly excited. "Yes! You know...I believe I'm right!" He was beginning to walk around her. His features, heavy and bloated were set in a serious expression. Then his eyes lighted, his thick eyebrows lifted and lips smiled once more. "Yes, I do believe that you might be...just might be a possibility for..." He made a motion with his hands. "Lift the skirt."

"What?"

"Lift the skirt a little. I want to see more of your legs. The part I'm thinking about...but first...let me see your legs."

Reluctantly she did as he asked.

"A little higher," he encouraged, his eyes beaming brightly. When she pulled it up beyond her knees he urged just a little higher, still.

"The dress won't go any higher!" she told him.

28

He shrugged, as if it really didn't matter and then eyed the top of her dress. "Pull it off the shoulders a little more. I just want to get the effect."

She hesitated.

"Don't be afraid. I just want...after all we're adults and I'm used to seeing women...well..." He reached out and placed his hands on her shoulders, pulling the top of the dress downwards. When it was almost off her bra-line he stopped. "Yes...I do think that maybe you would be good for the..."

He broke off for a second. Looked at his watch and then sighed sadly. "I didn't realize how late it was."

He went around to his desk and leaned over toward the small intercom.

"Call off appointments for the afternoon!" he said

Then he turned in her direction. "I want to get to know you better. How about lunch?"

She felt that fluttering warning. But now things were going so well, she couldn't take the chance of ruining them and her chances for even a bigger part, than the one she'd come for.

"You know, Norma...you don't mind me calling you that do you?"

"No."

"And you call me Walt...well, anyway, if things work out...I mean—if, after I know you a bit better, you still seem right for the part...well, it is a lot bigger and has several lines. You see the woman I have in mind is a sorta sexy thing..."

He led her out of the office, out of the building and then to a car in the studio parking lot. About fifteen minutes later they were at an expensive restaurant which featured dim lights and atmosphere spiced by cocktails and dinner type meals.

After the first martini she didn't feel as nervous. After the second, she almost felt at home. She was beginning to almost like this man.

She didn't even mind it when he took her hands in his and started fondling them. "You know, Norma, I'm beginning to think that you're just right for this part. You have the figure. And the personality. I never saw three martinis bring out such a lively personality in a person before."

She laughed. "Well, martinis always went to my head." For some reason her voice was low and throaty. She didn't mention that martinis also had a direct effect on her more basic sexual drives. But even fifty cocktails would never make Walter Bayles attractive to her. He just wasn't her type.

His hand moved up her arm. "You have very nice flesh," he told her. "I've always had a weakness for a woman with silky white flesh."

She just smiled her reaction to that comment. She didn't like where the conversation was heading.

"You know, the more I look at you, the more I'm sure you'd be good for this part." He hesitated a little and then went on. "In fact, I want you to do a little reading for me. Would you?"

She felt a sharp thrill of excitement. He was really considering her. It looked like she was in. And for the first time since she had come to Hollywood, she could see a future of shining successes and her name in lights. The thrill shivered through her whole frame. "Oh, *yes*. Anything."

He nodded and then in a fatherly manner patted her hand.

"Good...good!"

After a moment he got the waiter's attention. They ordered their lunch and the conversation continued in a different direction. After the meal was finished he ordered another cock-tail for each of them. The conversation slowly drifted back to the part she was supposed to try for.

"My place is just ways from here. The script is there."

She was too mentally foggy to really get the full meaning of that sentence.

Twenty minutes later she realized what he had said. His place was an expensive apartment. The moment the door was shut he stepped over to a small bar in the corner of room. A few seconds later they were sitting on a large sofa, two strong martinis on the small coffee table before them. Now, she realized, she was about to be forced to make the biggest decision of her life.

30

But he didn't make a pass. Instead, he actually brought forth a script and opened it to a page which he had marked. "Read this part...and I'll play the man."

She looked at the script. It was a love scene between the lead and a sexy young pick-up. The setting was an apartment much like the one they were now at. Both characters were sitting on a sofa with two martinis in front of them.

She looked up at him and raised her eyebrows. "Quite...similar."

He only smiled, without saying anything about that. "Just read the lines. I'll be the man..."

She started reading: "But, Mr. Carson, I'm just not that type of woman!"

He read the man's part, leaning closer to her so that he could see his lines. "Then why did you come to my apartment?"

"I don't see what that has to do with it..."

"Oh, come now! We're not children. You didn't really expect to just come up to see...well, after all, you're a woman and I'm a man!"

"That's just it!"

"And what is that supposed to mean?"

"That I think maybe *I* should leave...that's what it means!"

"Wonderful! Wonderful!" he told her, excitedly patting her leg. The action seemed so normal and natural and unconscious that she didn't bother to stop him. After a moment it lay there. "Read on..."

"And I'm leaving, right now!"

At this point the script called for the man to reach for the woman and pull her into a clinch. Much to her surprise, Bayles did exactly what the script called for. His eyes looked deep into hers. "You are lovely. So very lovely!" he told her. His voice was husky with emotion. His hands slid around her back.

That's when she realized that he wasn't playing a part anymore. He wasn't acting. This was for real. And he had so cleverly done it that everything seemed too far out of hand to *even* stop.

She struggled slightly to be free of him, but he didn't let

31

go. "Please, Mr. Bayles!"

He looked at her strangely for a moment and then laughed.

"I'm sorry. I got all worked up about the part and about you...you are lovely!"

She looked at the script. The action read that she was supposed to be grabbed by the man and then struggle; during which time he would finally convince her to give in.

"I'd like you to try this part of the scene. Remember that it's just acting. Nothing more!"

She gulped. Frantically her mind was trying to think of a way or reason out of acting that part of the script. There wasn't any logical reason. If she wanted to convince him that she was professional, then she'd have to go on through with it. Anyway, she realized, it was just acting.

His arms were still around her he pulled her to him. For a moment their lips actually touched. He froze. She could see a strange light in his eyes. The he pulled her harder to him. His mouth opened.

Then she realized that he actually was planning to continue on through. He was not in the least acting. And neither was she.

She struggled desperately. But he was stronger and, worst of all, he knew how to make a woman want a man. He knew what was necessary to spark passion.

It was almost pleasant at first; after it had started she couldn't have cared who she was with.

And like in the script, she finally stopped her physical and mental struggles, unable to control her need and desire. But, unlike the script, there was nobody to stop them.

Nobody said: "Cut!"

Afterwards, he very convincingly apologized to her. "I'm terrible sorry. I don't know what ever came over me. It was you. You're just about the most beautiful woman I've seen for a long time."

His words and actions were those of a gentleman. And after he drove her to the studio, and left her at her car, she wasn't really quite sure what to believe about him. He'd told her that he would call her agent the next morning and let him know what he had decided. It sounded and seemed odd to her, but she wasn't in any position to argue.

One thing she was sure about, though: she was just numb, mentally, physically and emotionally.

* * * * * * *

Walt Bayles was sitting at his desk the next morning, thinking about the joys of Norma Fosse's body *She had certainly fallen for that bigger part routine,* he laughed inwardly to himself. *But then, most women fell for the bit. Take them to lunch, give them a few cocktails and then offer to give them a reading at the apartment. The old script...it was certainly serving its purpose!*

He looked at the phone on his desk. She had been quite good! Such a beautiful body...it might be nice having her around.

He eyed the phone for a little longer. All he'd have to do is give her that Denton role she'd originally come to be interviewed for, and if she treated him right he could always have a few lines added for her.

It was the idea of her treating him right, like she had the afternoon before, that caused him to reach for the phone and call her agent.

And there was always one thing that he had always known from experience: A young woman gets better and better—more relaxed—as she has more and more interviews.

Maybe he'd make arrangements to call her up for another reading that evening.

That was a good idea!

He dialed her agent's number and waited, almost breathlessly.

&FITTE THE SIXTH&

There's a warning here, I suppose. You never can tell what you might find when you go to some cheap bar with the idea of getting a woman to take home. Sometimes it actually works out to everybody's benefit. Sometimes not.

A POCKET FULL OF PLEASURE&

They were out to have a ball, and Larry Clanton needed a blowout It had been several weeks since he'd had a woman, and now he planned an end to all that. His buddy, Glenn, had come into town that day and now they were out on the town.

The bar was one of those cheap places that featured rock and roll and twist and easy pick-ups. Larry and Glenn were sitting at a small table, looking over the young crop of female charmers, most of whom weren't what a man would call knock-outs.

Then suddenly two women stepped into the place, sat down at the bar and ordered drinks. Taking a deep, startled breath and blowing it out, Larry hissed in excitement. "Paydirt I think!" He pointed out the two women. "Take a look at those two broads! Now *they* should be easy pickings for a couple of guys with a few bills!"

Glenn turned and stared, his dark eyes becoming wide and his thick lips thinning out into a crooked grin.

One was a small, compact blonde, and from their view she looked like she had more than the right curves to excite any male animal. The other, dark haired, was slightly thinner, but still an eye-catcher. The angle showed only their profiles.

"Why not?" Glenn observed. "That's what we're out on the night for—and anyway, they look just like the kind that would fly high with a couple of guys like us!"

"Right!"

Larry motioned to one of the cocktail girls and then, handing her a five dollar bill, he whispered in the woman's ear. "Those two ladies, see if they would like to come over for a drink!"

"Yes, sir," the woman replied, grinning and starting across the smoky room.

They watched as she approached the two women in question and made the offer, pointing them out a moment later.

The blonde leaned closer to the dark haired girl, and they carried on a short conversation. Then abruptly they stood and started across the crowded saloon.

"Hello," Larry greeted, standing and indicating a chair toward the thinner, dark haired woman, ignoring the blonde, who was more Glenn's type. "My name's Larry, and this is Glenn."

They smiled and the blonde spoke: "Jean—that's me. And this is Gloria."

Larry turned to Gloria and gave her a warm smile, looking up and down her full, seductive figure packaged into a black sheath dress. The low cut neckline revealed that what she seemed to have from a distance was plenty real enough.

He extended his hand to help her into a chair and the feel of her fingers was silky and smooth and they gave a little squeeze against his.

"Well, now that we're old friends, what do you want to drink?" Glenn offered.

The conversation was, for a short time, stilted after the girls had ordered their drinks, but that wasn't the important thing, because each couple was giving each other the once-over. It began with simple glances, then a few moments later Larry was aware of a knee gently pressing into his. In response he reached for Gloria's hand, which eagerly clung to his.

After the first drinks the girls became a little more outward about their real interests, which were boldly expressed when Jean bluntly suggested: "You know, boys, this place is a drag! Why don't we go someplace else?"

Before either Larry or Glenn could say anything to that, Gloria took the ball: "We could go to a place I know of. Just around the corner. A hotel. I have a room there...to be truthful!" She giggled at the confession. "What do you say, boys?"

This was easier than they had expected! Larry thought, anxiously. Glenn answered for them:

"Sure thing, girls!"

Gloria took them to a small, cheap hotel. The room was a double, living and bed. She had a couple of bottles on the sink, and she quickly mixed drinks, then set the room lighting down to dim, so that it seemed as if only the moon was glowing through the room. Again the conversation lagged, but not the action.

The drinks were half finished before Larry had Gloria snuggling in his arm, feeling the warmth of her begin to get a little fiery. He was well aware of her breathing, which was becoming slightly shorter and faster and heavier.

"What do you girls do for a living?" Larry inquired, suddenly wondering exactly what two beautiful women might be doing, giving themselves so freely and easily. *Kicks, obviously,* he thought.

"Oh, a little of this and a little of that," Gloria stated, wiggling closer to Larry. "Let's not talk about *that*—don't you have more interesting things to do?"

The question was a leading one, and meant to be, and developed further by one simple fact:

Gloria's hand had slipped to his thigh, and the fingers slid subtly along the surface.

It took Larry a few seconds before he was sure that he had enough control over his voice to respond to her opening caress. Finally he managed, in a much too husky voice, to say: "Where does that doorway lead to?" The question was purposely innocent. He pointed to what he knew was the entrance to a bedroom.

She snickered gaily and then quickly stood, taking hold

of his hand and squeezing the fingers warmly. "Want to find out?"

He didn't answer that with words, but stood and started after her across the living room and through the door. Gloria closed it after her.

"See?" she asked, huskily. "Just what you were looking for, wasn't it?"

Larry only nodded and reached for the anxious bundle of womanhood, attempting to pull her into his arms.

She avoided him. "Not so fast!" she giggled, her eyes flashing, and her face brightening into a smile. "Wait a second."

For a moment she just stood there, staring at him, and then she reached quickly around her back and a moment later her dress slipped soundlessly down to the floor around her feet.

"Let's do it right—right from the start!" she told him, starting to unclasp her bra.

He watched, fascinated, as she undressed quickly and then was a little startled when she gazed up at him, irritation showing on her pretty little features.

"What's with you?" she demanded. "Get undressed!"

Laughing, he did as she bid and then she moved toward the bed in an animal-like stride and slid down on the top of it. Lying on her back, she waited for him to come to her. It didn't take long, because he was more than eagerly excited to clamp that lovely form against his own.

Fairly throwing his pants to one side, Larry moved to the bed and slid down next to the woman. The pure animal excitement of her full luscious body had burned him beyond the point of wanting to wait, even for one moment, to grip her to him.

Her high, pointed breasts swelled up against his chest, moving restlessly, their rigid nipples pressing and biting into him. She squirmed as she blended herself against him. Their lips met, violently, open and moist. He felt the stab of her tongue surge deep into his mouth, darting anxiously against his.

For a long time they held each other that way and then her hands tugged on his head and her lips moved away. The direction of her urging fingers left no doubt in his mind where she wanted him to kiss her, next. His lips submerged in hers. She responded against him with a convulsive shudder.

Later they moved exhaustedly away from one another, but after awhile it started again, wonderfully, excitingly, more exhaustingly She was a wonderful lover and this time, when she was finished, he fell back against the pillow and sleep clouded over his consciousness.

Larry awoke with a dry taste in his mouth and turned to reach for Gloria. She wasn't there!

Shock moved through him like he'd been plunged into the wall socket, and for a moment he couldn't organize his thoughts

Then leaping from the bed and moving to the other room, he saw Glenn lying on the sofa, sleeping. But no Gloria or Jean.

"Glenn!" he shouted, shaking his friend's shoulder. *"Glenn!* Wake up!"

Glenn moved and then swung his body to a sitting position on the sofa. "What is it?"

"The girls aren't here!"

"What the damnation?"

"Check your wallet."

The two of them checked through their belongings. Glenn shouted only a split second before Larry. "That little creep!"

"The whores!" Larry's voice exploded into the room.

"The same thing?" Glenn asked. "All the money gone?"

Larry nodded, tight lipped. "Guess we found out what they do for a living!"

For a moment the two looked at each other and then suddenly broke into a grin. A moment later they were laughing.

"There...we're suckered!" Glenn observed, sobering. "How much did they take you for?"

"About twelve dollars!"

"You were lucky. Me—it cost twenty-five. And no bed to boot!"

"Well, thinking it over—maybe Gloria might have been

worth the twelve dollars, and a lot more—at that!"

Glenn grinned half crookedly. "Okay—so they got a little money out of it. And we got a little fun and games! Maybe it *was* worth it. At least the lesson is worth it. Pickups are for the whores!"

ഔFITTE THE SEVENTHര

Well, if you are going to deal with prostitution and all that, and some of these stories certainly, at best, linger over this very subject, one way or another, then maybe it might be smart to consider an argument…

*IN DEFENSE OF PROSTITUTION*ര

They call it the "world's oldest profession" and label it as something dirty and immoral. It's been condemned socially for so long that it is impossible to remember when it was embraced by all and accepted as a part of life. It is illegal in the United States, and many countries in the world at least restricted. The so-called "red-light" districts, where a series of "houses" would line the street for the direct purpose of selling a woman's body for an evening to any man might desire to buy her services, are outlawed. The wild west days are over. Today the only way for men to find a woman who is willing to sell herself physically to him for a few hours of pleasure is by going to a cheap bar, or by finding a contact to a "call-girl". And escort service. It isn't easy, it isn't cheap and it isn't legal! And some say it isn't moral, either!

We're not concerned with the morality—purely the practical side of the subject.

In support of the legal and moral side of the argument it should be pointed out that they have a strong case.

Most prostitutes come from broken families, poor families, or where the mother and father are unhappy together or drink to excess, or where there is illegitimacy. Many come

40

from the tragedy of having been seduced at a very early age, either by friend or father or stepfather. The fact is that most girls get into prostitution because of an *early environment* which *was* inducive to seeking a quick and easy escape. Poverty, drug addiction and physical threats, can cause a girl to turn to this way of making a living. Sometimes it is simply survival. Runaways get trapped in the big city cesspool that won't let them escape: sell their bodies or starve. By the time that they have been in their profession long enough to become expert in the arts of pleasing a man for money, more than 80% will have been infect by some form of venereal disease. Many of these women die prematurely of these diseases or because of mental disorders created as a direct result of their professional experience. (2006 note: and AIDS demands the use of condoms for safe sex.) This is the ugly side. The elements which would shock any thinking person.

Yet there are other considerations to take into account. One point is that while prostitution has its built-in bad points, it helps to solve many other problems. The Christian theologian, Saint Augustine, after the fall of Rome, believed that if prostitution were eliminated it would cause far worse forms of perversion, vice and immorality, so, in his own belief, it was a lesser evil.

Interesting conclusion.

Society has tried to rule it out many times in history but never managed to do so. It couldn't be stopped in the fifteenth or sixteenth centuries any more than it has been stopped today. Paris, during this period, had orders that all prostitutes be flogged and shaved bald and placed into exile for life, without rights of a trial, and yet they couldn't stop it.

Today the only thing which laws against prostitution have been able to do is create a new form which is called the "call girl". And the price for this woman's services ranges from *$25* to $500 a night! (And far more in 2006.) All this has done is to make it impossible for the young man on the street to easily obtain a woman's services —and places prostitution either in the streets or on a large nationwide big-business scale. Big business hires women to "please" out-of-town clients so they will give the orders to their company. It is all handled in a delicate way—but it is simple prostitution at high prices.

What are the reasons for man to seek out a woman for the night? Why will somebody be willing to pay money for a woman's entertainment? And more important, why is prostitution so very important to society and young men *and* women?

Let's take a typical case of the sensitive young man who believes in the standard "accepted" social moral code. Which is? That there should be *no* sexual relations between a man and a woman until the wedding night.

It is a popular belief that repressing the sexual urge over a period of time can cause a man to be unable to perform the sex act. Be that as it may, one harm it can do is to make things awkward on that most important night when he takes his bride in his arms and is expected to be a GREAT lover. *Without experience!* He is expected to caress her with expert care, to build the desires and passions in her virginal body to the peak of ecstasy and then finish this first experience in making love as if he had done it all his life and knew exactly what he was doing. The question which comes to mind quite vividly is: how many women have enjoyed the first sexual experience—even with a *skilled* partner? And what's more: what is the young bride's reaction to a husband who turns out to be awkward, inexperienced and unable to complete a sexual act? It is a recorded fact that many—if not *most*— divorces are caused because of sexual mismatching or "mental cruelty," as it is many times called—which means that the husband, for one reason or another, was unable to develop a satisfactory relationship in the bed chambers with his wife. Many women live their lives in such a marriage with men who never give them sexual satisfaction; some cheat, some simply live sexless lives.

We won't deal with the fact that few women are virgins on their wedding night, or than the very idea of remaining a virgin is considered, in some circles, as rigidly outdated. Regardless of all these factors in modern times, the reality is that we live in a world of true believers who think that sex is basically for building family, rather than pure pleasure and daughters are still taught to save it for their wedding night. The public stance, even the legal structure in many countries and societies place a rigid price tag on virginity for unmarried women. So, let us bypass all that and consider what prostitution can do for society in general.

Sure, it is true that many couples manage to *learn* together but how many others never get this far?

How many so-called "frigid" wives are merely women who have husbands unable to excite their desires and bodies to the point where they get sexual pleasure during the act?

If a young man had a way to learn, before marriage— *without* the process of seducing as many young girls as he was able to—the arts of love making, many of these problems would he solved *before the wedding night!* And there are many experienced men—but their experience has come from seducing young women and learning while taking the virginity of their bodies. How much worse is this than seeking out an expensive prostitute and learning "what the score is" from one who knows the ways of sex?

But this is merely one side of the defense for prostitution

What about the man who is not married? What should he do to relieve the needs of his body? Seduce women for the mere pleasure of seeing how many he can have? Or would it be better if he could seek out a prostitute, pay for her services and then leave? Some would suggest that is far more moral to seek a professional rather than taking advantage of some women who might not want to be sexually active with her date.

Seduction isn't rape; but it can be a form of pressure that breaks down the reluctance of some women not sophisticated enough to simply say "No" and mean it.

What about sexual crimes?

Would there be as many if there was legal prostitution? It is provable fact that in countries where prostitution is legal, there are less sexual crimes, almost to the point where they aren't even heard of!

How many young girls have not only lost their virginity in a sordid back-seat-of-a-car-seduction, but also ended with bearing an unwanted child? Is this what the law is trying to aid by making it impossible for a young man to find out what sex is all about with a professional prostitute. Isn't there some realistic way to avoid such tragic "accidents"? Sure, sexual education on a grand scale might help. But even then, there is a place for prostitution even in this social equation.

Wouldn't it be much better for a young man to satisfy his natural and normal interest in his body and sexual urges with the help of a professional prostitute instead of with some young girl his own age whom he takes advantage of?

There is no question about the fact that neither solution is really desirable. Neither pro nor con leads to Utopia! Yet where is the answer? What solution could be suggested which is *better* than having legal prostitution to solve the sexual side of American life? A defense for prostitution is merely an argument against the closed-mind attitudes of many people who say that sex isn't here, that it isn't a problem, and that people shouldn't indulge in it! And there are no children born out of wedlock, and teenage pregnancy doesn't exist.

It is impossible to curb the sexual urge; it is a basic part of our nature and needs to be realistically guided and realistically dealt with in a way that is the least damning and damaging to people and society at large.

It is a defense for the *only* solution which we have at the present for the realistic problem of the need for young men to learn something about the sexual side of life without harming themselves or others in the process. Better with a professional than seducing virgins. The idea of children learning from other inexperienced children is frightening. And that's what happens every day. Young boys doing their best to get the girl to do it with them. Such activity is a reality, but it is, at the same time, a damning one, and if prostitution was widely accepted it might very well help to cut down the numbers of illegitimate births.

The fact is that no matter what the law reads it can never, has never, and will never make prostitution stop existing. People have tried to stop it throughout history and failed. It existed in ancient times, before Rome and it was a natural part of that Empire. And it continues to exist. Where there is a demand, there will be a product to fulfill that demand! Enough men want the services of prostitutes—and because of that they will be with us until another solution has been presented for our needs.

Saying it is wrong, evil and immoral, doesn't change the fact that there is a basic need for prostitution in the scheme of things—*like it or not!* And until that time when the need for it stops and another solution is offered, there will be men to buy, women to sell, and all the shouting and all the legal double-talk will never change the fact that it is here to stay!

Right or wrong! Moral or immoral!

Face the truth!

There is a defense for prostitution!

✍FITTE THE EIGHTH✎

Ah, can you believe it, a detective story…of sorts! Well, our hero here, in this bit of fluff, is out to get his man…er…girl! Well, maybe both! But would he take…

BRIBERY IN FLESH✎

All Carter knew was that he had to find a pretty blonde girl, and that the rest would follow.

"Get her, and you get the man!" the Chief had said, when he had assigned the case to him. Al Carter, detective in charge of the narcotics squad.

He hadn't gotten a lead on her until the night before. It had been a long and tiring search, covering several weeks of footwork. But now he was on the trail, and the old hunter's blood was pulsing through his eager veins.

She was called *Lazy Daisy*, and was a singer at a small club which featured a lot of sex and little talent. It was a good thing for "Lazy" because he couldn't even follow the tunes she sang. Either he was square to her kind of jazz, or she just couldn't sing.

After the first show, he had gone backstage to the dressing room. She was friendly, but not too informative.

"What can I do for you?" she asked after he shown his badge and introduced himself.

"You know where I can find Ricker...Dave Ricker?" he asked, looking over the twin balls of flesh which pushed out the front of her low cut dress.

"Davy? I ain't seen him for weeks. He took a dive when

things got hot!" She was giving him the eager eye. "What you want him for?"

"Twelve guesses, honey!" he said, moving closer until the pointed balloons were only inches from his chest. It was hard not to grab hold of her, and the way she was giving him the come-on didn't make anything easier.

"Well, hon, I don't know where he's padded out...but if you got some time off some evening...I might be able to...well …"

He got the message, but didn't have the time. Not right then.

He was about to leave when something on her dresser caught his eye. It was nothing worthy of attention, unless they knew something about Ricker, and the man's habits. It was a little piece of paper, sorta twisted. Twisted the way that Ricker had of nervously mangling hits of loose paper.

He acted like he hadn't seen it, and then walked calmly out. He'd have to tail Miss Lazy; she knew where Davy was.

It was well past 2:30 AM before the girl left the club. She walked to a car in the parking lot, started the engine. He let her get about a block away before he started his sedan, and followed. He kept the same distance throughout the long drive over the night city. Everything seemed to be sleeping except the two cars. And finally the vehicle in front of him came to a stop before a small homey house. He drove on past, circled a block and parked the car. He got out, and walked back to where she had parked.

Carefully he crept up to the house. There was a light on in the window facing the front porch. Silently he moved forward, and he finally stood on the porch looking in.

The girl was lying on a couch, completely naked. Her pert, well-formed breasts were pointed up toward the ceiling, her face laughing nervously as she watched Ricker, undressing.

It was perfect! He could walk in on them without their even knowing he was near.

The man lay down next to her, caressing her breasts and stomach, as their lips met. For a long moment Al Carter watched, fascinated by the sex play, the writhing of the woman's body as it enjoyed the pleasure-filled touch. Then suddenly they locked together in a violent shuddering vice. He legs wrapped around his in their agony of passion. Even from where he was, Carter could hear their sighs of explosive, pain-filled pleasure.

With a grunt he smashed the window glass with his gun, gripped the latch, and after a moment of struggle, lifted the frame.

"Just stay where you are!" he commanded the two lovers as he climbed into the room.

In that moment of balance, when he was just getting both feet planted on the floor, the man rose, and with incredible speed pulled the girl in front of his body.

"You shoot and she gets it!" he cried savagely, backing up toward a table, which Carter could see had a gun on it. With a leap he rushed the two.

Ricker pushed the girl directly at him, and the impact of her body almost knocked him over. She grappled with Carter, trying to help her boy friend. He smashed her in the face with the flat of the gun, and she slid to the floor out of his way. He had to get at the man. Ricker wouldn't stop at killing him.

"Don't move!" he shouted. But the young hood jumped forward before Carter could do anything. A fist smashed into his face, then strong fingers twisted his arm. He heard a snapping sound.

At first he thought a bone had been broken, then realized. The sound had been his gun falling to the floor.

The other man was reaching for his weapon. Carter kicked out at Ricker's face, connecting in a bone-crushing force that sent the hood flying across the room to hit the far wall with a thud.

Carter looked around. Two naked lovers completely knocked cold.

He reached for the phone, pocketing his gun. He got as far as the second number when a body rammed into him. He fell to the floor, grappling with the writhing thing on his back. Then something hit the back of his head and dimness flooded out his brain.

He ebbed back to consciousness.

Light blurted into his vision. He looked around.

"Well, copper," Ricker said, looking down at him, then slapping him across the face. "I see you're back with us!" The man was fully dressed.

"What are you going to do with him?" asked a woman's voice.

"I don't rightly know, Ruthie!" Ricker said, looking over his shoulder.

Carter followed the man's gaze. Miss Lucy Daisy was standing in the middle of the room, fear and concern working into a distorted image. "You...you aren't going to do anything foolish...I mean...not kill him?

"Don't be square!" Ricker snapped.

"Davy...don't say that..." she cried, moving closer to the couch on which Carter was lying.

"Look, I can't have him hanging around to...well I'm hot, and all they have to do is scent my trail and I'll fry!" he shouted, making a threatening step toward her.

It was Carter's chance. Attention was directed away from him. With all the strength he could force into the blow, he hammered his hand at the side of the man's neck. Richer crumpled to the floor.

The girl looked from Crater to the obviously dead form of her lover. Then fear filled her eyes again as she looked back at the detective. "What...what are you...you going to do to me...I...I didn't no nothing!"

He looked long and hard at her. She hadn't done much, outside of helping a fugitive of the law.

Her expression changed suddenly. It became all sweetness and hot tropical passion. Moving up close to him she slid her arms around his neck, caressing the back of his head, before he could do anything to stop her.

"You...you don't want to turn me in...do you?" she murmured in a husky voice, pressing her hips against his, and rotating them hard and seductively.

His blood burned. She was one hell of a lovely creature. Remembrance of those delightfully pert breasts, tipped with their pointed, rigid nipples, sent sparks of hot fire through his nervous system. He knew what she was offering him. It was obvious. And very temping. She crushed herself against him, and her lips moved onto his.

He felt the warm moistness of her tongue as it searched anxiously for his. And suddenly he realized that it was more than just the eager necessity of her getting a way out; she wanted him. He wanted her too.

What the hell! he thought, lifting her bodily and carrying her to the sofa. He could take her now, promising anything, and turn her in later.

In a wildly exciting series of actions. they helped each other undress, then locked in a vice-like writhing hardness to each other.

Her tongue was a darting snake in his mouth, and he fell into a pit of burning agony of ecstasy, as he matched her eagerness. Her breasts squirmed up against his fingers, quivering and oiled with sweat. Then in a rhythmic explosion of action, they exploited each other's bodies.

Afterwards he looked down at her. She was smiling. "I knew you'd be good...oh, so good!" she sighed, pulling his head down to her neck. He could feel the pulse of blood rushing through her veins as he kissed the creamy white smoothness of that throbbing throat.

"You...you won't turn me in...will you?" she asked, pushing her stomach against his. He felt a convulsive ripple of the muscles in her body. "No...don't...I...want you...more and more..." she sighed. And he knew what she meant.

She would be his, for the price of silence.

Suddenly they were kissing again. They were making violent, explosive love. Their bodies were mingling, and the sweat of lovers' excitement united them again.

No, he wouldn't turn in a woman like her...he couldn't! Her bribery in flesh was just too inviting, too hot, too everything. No. How could he turn her in? She was his for the taking! Any time he wanted. Now that was some bribery! In the flesh!

෨FITTE THE NINTHଔ

I don't know. What does a girl do when faced with rape? Does she fight back? Or does she surrender? Or, possibly, fake it with the beast who holds her helpless? This is a nasty little bit of fluff that was designed to tell the story of a woman who was ...

*PICKED UP TO BE RAPED*ଔ

It took her several seconds to react; or realize what was happening.

Then it was too late.

One moment she was alone on the street; the next second a car pulled up, and a dark figure jumped out at her.

She was grabbed by the arm, then pulled toward the open car door.

"You be quiet, baby!" a rasping voice snapped at her, as she was shoved into the front seat. "Don't make a sound, or I'll bat your brains out!"

The man leaned toward her, and his face was large and ugly. He took hold of her arm, squeezing it hard, until tears came to her eyes.

"You don't have to hurt me...I'll be quiet!" she whimpered.

"Good!" The hand moved down to her thigh, pressing the inside of it.

The touch sent a sickening chill through her, running the full length of her nervous system.

"We're just going for a little ride." He grinned at her. A

large ugly grin spread his thick lips out into thin lines, outlining crooked teeth.

Turning from her, he put the car into gear and it moved forward.

As soon as they were driving safely along the highway, he slid his hand down to her thigh again.

She cringed from it; horrified.

God, how had this happened to me, she cried inwardly.

She had always wondered what it might be like to be picked up by a stranger, who intended to seduce—or rape—her. But now she knew and she didn't like it!

"Oh, please mister, let me out. Please, don't!" She tried to move away; to disengage that crawling thing on her leg. But it clamped harder, digging deep into her flesh, ripping the skirt slightly.

Her voice choked in pain.

"Please...please...you're hurting me...or God, *please!*"

"Just you get over here, *closer!*" the man demanded, turning to look at her.

His hand pressed harder, pulling her leg toward him. Pain coughed in her throat. She slid closer to him.

Sobs moved her chest up and down. Tears of pain and terror filled her eyes. Her head felt dizzy. She had to fight to keep from fainting.

His fingers slid down between her legs.

She screamed; pulling away.

Her hands flung out at him. She struck his arm, and then aimed at his face.

He cursed. Yelled for her to stop. He pulled his hand away from her legs and smashed it against her chest.

She collapsed in pain. Her breasts were paralyzed in agony.

Another fist flung at her, hitting her leg; it swung again, smashing into her face.

She screamed and cringed, moving away from that terrible beating first.

"Damn you. You little bitch!" he swore. "That'll teach you to hit me. I should kill you for that, you bitch!"

She folded her face in her hands and cried. She wished she was dead; yet was afraid, at the same time, he would kill her.

Her leg hurt terribly, and her chest throbbed. Her head spun dizzily where he had hit it.

How long they drove she did not know. She was in her own world of terror and fear. She was horrified. Agonized. Scared.

At last the ride came to an end.

They were in a dark, wooded, lonely road.

In the country.

Alone.

The man turned toward her.

"Come over here, baby!" he demanded, grinning.

She hardly heard his words. She was deafened with fear. Almost blinded with it. She could not move.

"Damn you, come over here!" he screamed, leaning toward her. His hand reached out, grabbed hold of the top of her dress, and pulled downward, exposing her chest.

His fingers grabbed hold of her brassiere and yanked it aside, exposing her breasts. Her body was pulled toward him.

"That's the baby." He clutched her in his arms, squeezing her to him.

She was sick.

Her whole body was shaking.

His mouth moved toward hers. She tried to pull away; but couldn't. She struggled to free her arms. She fought to get out of his grasp. But he held her tight.

His lips crushed against hers violently.

They were big and moist. They parted. His hand pulled open her mouth.

A scream uttered from her. His tongue pushed past her teeth, licking the cavity behind them.

She gagged. Her stomach retched. A sickening acid-like fluid exploded up her throat, flooding her mouth.

She was sick.

He pulled away with disgust. His hand slapped across her face.

She choked.

Her whole body was convulsively retching.

"Damn you...damn you!" he bellowed, slapping her

53

again and again.

Something snapped inside her.

She lost her sickness. Her mind became hard with mad fury, her hands, arms, legs reacted swiftly; automatically.

She beat at his face, his chest and his body.

Her fists smashed down at his legs. Between them. Crushed at his face, until he began to yell in pain and terror. He struggled to be free of her.

Desperately his hands flung out. A fist connected on her jaw. She staggered backward, falling against the far door. Her head struck it, and she felt dizzy. Blackness started to ebb over her.

She struggled for awareness.

She had to keep alert.

There was no telling what he might do to her.

Suddenly she was aware of a rough hand caressing her body. A pair of lips touching her flesh.

She shuddered.

Awareness came.

He was leaning over her.

She trembled with nausea.

She knew she could not out hit him. He was too strong. There had to be some other way. She needed something hard to hit him with.

She looked desperately around, fully conscious of his searching fingers, and hungry moist mouth.

What seemed hours of hell were but seconds.

She saw her purse on the floor. It was hard, with a metal frame around it. The purse was just within reach, but she didn't dare move for fear of him hitting her again. Unless she made him think...

It would be necessary to be very convincing; even to convincing herself she was liking what the man was about to do. This had to be the best acting she had ever done. Women were known to fake it, so now she would have to learn how. Just let herself experience...without mental instructions to block all pleasure centers. She tried to open them up, to attempt, at least, to feel something more than just pain, fear, terror.

Get the mind going and the body will follow! Imagine

this is a date, somebody she's madly in love with, somebody she really wanted to be with in a totally intimate way. Imagine he's her lover. Imagine for your very life!

Swallowing hard, and mentally trying to detach herself, she let a sigh utter from her mouth. She tried to make it sound like a thrilling murmur. And at the same time she moved her body upwards, as if seeking to get closer to him. She let a tremor run through her.

Suddenly she became aware of his body. Of his mouth. Of the thrilling touch of his hands.

They were all caressing. They were soft. Delightful.

A thrill passed through her.

His fingers pressed up to her breasts; touching them excitingly. His face moved to her lips, pressing his open mouth to them; hers was beginning to open...her arms were sliding around his body.

She felt excited all over. Her skin was flaming. She quivered with sudden delightful passion. Her breath was heavy.

His kisses were wonderfully thrilling. And she was returning them with an exploding fire she had never realized was in her.

They were lying full length on the car seat, and he pressed his body hard to hers.

She suddenly became numb.

What was she doing?

God, her mind screamed...

In a furor of terror her hand reached out, searching for the purse.

Where was it?

Oh God, but he was exciting.

His hands.

His tongue.

His body.

She was burning up.

She felt the hard rim of metal that encircled the edge of her purse. Her fingers clamped around it. Gripping it hard.

His hand touched her breast. His lips were sucking violently on her mouth.

It was thrilling. More than resistance could stand up to.

Let him continue, just for a few moments longer.

Just one more moment.

Yes! Oh yes!

Her body burned with desire, and passion. It was on fire. Desiring. Stimulated.

One more moment, it cried desperately at her terrified brain.

With effort she forced her arms up above the man's head.

One second longer, her whole being screamed. Just one more caress; on more thrilling sensation.

And then…

The purse smashed down on the back of his head.

He was quiet.

It had worked! And she was free of the monster.

She smashed the shapeless purse once more into his bruised skull, and then collapsed backwards, exhausted.

ℬFITTE THE TENTHℛ

Cheating can be dangerous to all concerned. And certainly a nasty business when a mate discovers the truth about their spouse. In this case, we see a man who is determined to catch his wife in the very act! And that was costing him a lot of time and effort. But, in the long run, he figured it was worth it in order to get even with his...

*CHEATER WIFE!*ℛ

One thing that Guy Raymond didn't like was a cheater wife. A woman married a man, and she was supposed to be loyal. She wasn't supposed to step out on him.

That was not only his belief, but also the belief of many other people in the world, so you couldn't really blame him for doing what he did.

He had been watching his wife for weeks, keeping an eye on her; but she had played it real cool. He knew that she was seeing a lover, but the moment he started suspecting anything she must have been aware of it, because she didn't see the guy at all. Still, there was a time when she wouldn't be able to stand it any longer. So he really put it on for quite awhile, in such a way that she couldn't help but notice and be careful, then when he seemed to give the whole idea up, she became very confident.

That's when he caught them.

It had been pretty tough on him, naturally, because he had to keep such a careful watch, and there were other things to keep a person happy, outside of watching for your wife to

57

walk out on you to go into the arms of a lover.

After all, he had his hobby, which he didn't have time for while keeping an eye on his wife.

It was dark out the night he followed her from the house, up town toward the cheap district. She had her car, and he had his.

"I'm going to do some shopping with a girl friend of mine," she had said. He knew that that was a damn lie.

It was.

She went to an apartment house which was dirty, old, and ill kept.

Then up to a three room flat, as it turned out to be. He gave them a half hour, then he walked up and knocked on the door, which he had seen his wife go into earlier.

There was no answer

He knocked again.

Then again.

Louder and louder, until he was banging and pounding.

Finally he heard an angry voice call *dimly* from behind the wooden paneling. "Be right there..."

The door opened.

He didn't wait to be introduced. With one move, or thought, or warning he swung.

The man fell backwards

He followed the first blow with another and another until the man was only a crumpled mass of blood and flesh on the floor. Then he went to the bedroom.

Sure enough there his wife was, nude as can be in bed.

Alarm showed in her eyes. Terror in the way she pulled the covers up over her lovely body.

Fury was pounding in his guts. At that moment he could have killed her. Right then and there.

Then another thought occurred to him. A much better plan, with a lot more excitement in it.

In jerky motions he moved to the bedside pulled the covers aside and after sipping off his clothing lay down behind his wife.

He'd teach her to go to a lover. He'd teach her for sure.

And he did.

Never had she been so wild, so anxious so savage as she

was this evening. She bit, clawed, whimpered, moaned and screamed in the agony of ecstasy. The two of them were determined to be as cruel and savage as possible.

It was great.

Then he lifted her up in his arms, draped a robe around her shoulders and carried her out to his car, where he did the need to her again.

Once home he repeated the action.

She was overwhelmed. Delighted. Overjoyed. Thrilled.

The next morning she came into his arms, all love and kisses. "Do it to me...do it to me!" She sighed pushing her breast against his fingers and working them into that soft, giving, supple flesh ball.

She was wonderful. The best she had ever been before. At the very peak of their enjoyment she screamed: "Oh, God you're wonderful...wonderful..."

Later she promised never, never to cheat again.

"That's good," he exclaimed happily. He had made his point, and his wife.

Now back to his hobby.

That evening he called from work and told her that he wouldn't be back till late, that he had work to do at the office. She sounded disappointed, but begged him to be home as soon as possible. "I want you...I want you desperately."

He knew damn well she wanted him.

That evening he spent with the wife of an old buddy of his who was out of town.

His hobby?

Seducing as many married women as possible!

Naturally!

FLUFF, BY CHARLES NUETZEL

ಖFITTE THE ELEVENTHಞ

Sometimes it just ain't fair! Some people get the best jobs. Take this PI hired to check out a wild wife. And he was about to get more than he could possibly expect! He had been hired by her rich husband to prove she was a tramp. And that's exactly what he was doing—in spades!

BLACKMAIL REVERSEDಞ

It was a dirty business he was in. But there was nothing he could do about it now. It was too late to back out.

Of course there were compensations in the fact that she was a real doll. Beautiful. Mountainous breasts. Narrow waist, Round, circling hips. Full thighs and legs. Exciting, large hips.

He ran his hand along the full curve of her naked breasts, and felt the tingling excitement which made it quiver under his touch.

"You're nice," she murmured softly, looking up at him with her wide, green eyes. There was something in her inno- cent gaze, though, which puzzled. An almost mocking glint. He wondered about it.

Her lips parted slightly, and the pink wetness of her tongue moistened them until they glistened brightly in the moonlight. She was a mighty desirable woman.

He worked her mountains under his fingers again, this time more excitedly. She responded, quivering convulsively.

The couch felt cool under him, as he lay next to her. Ea- gerly he pressed closer to that soft velvet fullness of her fig-

60

ure.

"You are nice," she repeated, running her fingers in his hair.

He hoped the recorder was picking up her voice.

He felt a burning pain run thru him. A pain of anguished desire, which welled up from every nerve and cell in him. A burning, fiery pain.

It was a filthy racket...a hell of a way to make a living.

Yet, it had its good side, he thought, as he opened his palm over her large breast. It pressed anxiously up against his fingers.

"Oh, you are good..." she sighed, turning her body toward him, and squirming wildly next to his.

"Yes, baby...yes..." He reached his arms around her, drawing her closer, feeling the silken vibrancy of her flesh, as it crushed hard and warm...quivering and eager.

"Oh, take me...yes...take me some more..." she fairly yelled into the blackness of night. Her lips flooded over his like wild sucking things, with a violence that weakened and boiled him raw with desire. He worked his hands over her body with an eager, searching caress, feeling the sacred treasures which were so honestly being offered him.

Her lips sucked like moist silk on his ear lobe, and he felt the rough, delicate eagerness of her tongue as it worked between them.

"Some more..." she cried, over and over in a frantic repetition of a few minutes before, when they had been locked in the vice of their passionate lusts for the first time.

It was a true and tried saying that the second time was better than the first. But that was impossible. He couldn't see how her body could give more excitement than it had before, and thought it wasn't necessary. Since he had enough information on the recorder. But he had to find out. He couldn't stop now, even if he wanted to.

He was weak. Terribly tired and overcome.

Then it was over.

But she did not release her claw like grip upon him. She did not remove her body from his. She did not allow him to forget her hard nearness. Her body writhed. Her hips still worked on his. They were fiery. Her lips ran along his neck, and he felt the sting of her tongue and teeth under them. Her breasts quivered on his chest. They were gigantic swells that rose and fell under him.

"Again, honey, oh, again...you're so good...so good!" she sighed, breathing harder.

Those pumping breasts didn't stop their excited actions; and her hips started moving more wildly on his; her legs wrapped stronger around him; her arms frantically working on his back, the fingers her closer.

If she were a part of him she couldn't have gotten closer.

She was a hot fire. A burning well of energy which did not want to stop. She was violently working his body into a fever of heat that wanted to take her again and again. It demanded to have her...

He couldn't take much more. He had to stop. There was enough material on the tape machine by now.

After all, his job was finished. He had the proof that her husband wanted.

The recording was surely complete enough. There was more evidence than needed to put her in the hell where she belonged.

She was a wild force. The hottest sexual machine he had ever had. Pure volcanic fire.

And she was rippling over him like crazy.

He had the evidence so that he husband could get the divorce from her he wanted. She was a tramp, and he could prove it.

Rich men, well-to-do in business, can't afford to have wives who step out. Men who have married for money can't afford to get divorced and lose all that loot...on the other hand, if the wife was unfaithful...a tramp...maybe some other arrangements could be made. A high society girl who took up with any man she could pick up at a bar, like she had with him tonight...well...

But he couldn't stop now. He couldn't. The burning was too strong for him. She was wildly, faster and faster, fanning the flame she had started for the third time under him.

She stopped. Suddenly. Without warning. She was frozen. Ice. Unmoving.

"Now," she snapped, looking up coldly at him. "The recording...erase it...or..."

He was insane with passion. He was wild with hunger and demanding desire from her. He had to have her. He just had to.

He clawed at her breasts with his fingers, trying to work her to the fever pitch he was...the soft swells of supple flesh became cut and bruised. But she only laughed at him. Unresponsive. He cut her lips with his teeth in a choking demand for excitement to return.

It wouldn't.

"You little bitch..." he cursed.

"The recording...I know my husband hired you. I have a few people working for me, too. You kill the recording." She pushed him coldly away. Her beautiful lips smiled, mockingly. "Destroy the recordings, or give them to me, and I'll come back tomorrow...and show you a real good time...I like you a lot."

He was weak from shock. He trembled. He felt an ill grind in his guts that pounded over and over. His head was a pumping ache.

She walked over the closet and got her coat. Wrapping it around her, she gathered her clothing from the floor and walked out.

He knew he'd have to have her! There was no question in his mind.

She was sexier than anything he had ever known. And the promise of that excitement of her body those last few moments was too much for any man to ignore.

She'd get what she wanted.

And so would he.

ᔕᴏFITTE THE TWELFTHᔕᴏ

Some like it hot, some like it cold, some like it in the pot, nine days old—but in this little country story we discover a couple of people who discover, together, the pleasures of...

*A HOT DAY IN THE COUNTRY*ᔕᴏ

Sally Bankes rolled nervously on her bed, throwing off the covers, and rubbing her long slender arms real hard.

God, there must be something wrong with me, she thought, *I'm sexed all over.*

Her nerves felt raw and burning.

There must be something in the air.

It felt sexy.

Maybe it was the heat.

Irritably, she sat up.

What she needed was to be back in New York. This vacation stuff out in the country, where there weren't any men—at least not *her* kind—was dull as hell. She wished with all her body for one of her city boy friends.

Hell, face it, Sally...what you need is a little sex! Hell, a lot of sex.

She viciously clawed at her thighs and then with an angry sigh she got up and started dressing.

Right now any man would do.

Her whole body ached for a caressing male hand. She wanted one so much she could taste it.

If it weren't that country boys talked it up too much, she'd have gone out and gotten herself one a day ago. But a girl had to watch out for her reputation.

A city man, like the ones she ran around with, knew how to keep his mouth shut; and have one hell of a good time.

She'd give almost anything for one nice big city man right now, her body shivered horribly at the very thought of it.

What she needed was a walk; maybe that would calm her a bit.

She picked up her worn and tattered brassiere, and then shook her head: *It's too hot for you baby, anyway*

Boy, she sure needed some new underclothing

That was the trouble with working her way through college; she had to cut corners.

But she'd have to get new things, when she got back to the city; if she could afford it or not.

In disgust she thrust aside her panties too.

I'd like to go out just in the raw...but even here in the sticks someone might see her!

With an angry shrug of her shoulders she stepped into blue jeans, and pulled on a pink, man's style shirt.

* * * * * * *

Henry Forrest pressed the gas pedal savagely downwards.

This was one hell of a hot day to try selling anything, he cursed, directing his speeding car along the bumpy country road.

Normally he wouldn't be driving so fast over such a dangerously rough road. But he felt tired, hot and discouraged. Nothing seemed to be going right.

Too hot a day for making sales and that meant a lot of extra energy expended for nothing and it was just too hot to put up with it all.

He'd like to be in a bar in New York or in bed with a lovely blonde or redhead or who cared?

Anything would do; as long it was a girl.

Right at this moment he was angry with himself for having decided to work his way across country. No women, no fun, no nothing!

He had read a lot of stories about country girls in the national bare-breasted magazines like *Playbody*, but nothing had come his way and he wasn't so sure if he would be willing if it did.

It wasn't that he didn't want it; just that he was a little afraid of the country wench that might have a father or brother around just ready to force a shotgun wedding.

Some wide open country he was traveling through; no women, no sales, no nothing.

He'd been silly to think he could sell ladies underwear products out here in the hill country—hillbilly country

Of course, it didn't make too much difference, he had enough money to carry him to California; and there he could *always* stay in the land of the *stars*.

The road turned suddenly.

It was too sharp: too fast

Slamming on his brakes, he tried to slow down. The car swerved; balanced on two wheels and slid to stop just short of the trunk of a gigantic oak tree.

The breath was blasted away from his lungs. He felt numb and dazed. His guts were pounding like hammers. His head spun. His skin and muscles were shaking.

He didn't notice the girl until she pushed her head through the door window and peered curiously at him.

A vision from heaven?

No!

Heaven didn't make women *that* sexy.

He must be in hell.

He felt an urge to lean forward and kiss her full and exciting lips. They were moist, desirable, and kissable.

Her eyes, large and blue as the skies, studied him carefully.

"Are you all right?" she whispered as if her words might harm, or shatter him into nothingness.

She was trying to open the door. It was stuck and she struggled violently with it.

"I think so," he breathed out, hardly above a sigh. His stomach still felt shaken.

He tried to collect his thoughts.

It had been a close call; too close for his nervous system.

"I was walking in the fields...and I heard this horrible noise...gosh, I thought for sure somebody had gotten killed or something."

Her struggles with the door came to an abrupt halt as it swung suddenly outward, flinging her to the ground, and dumping Henry, who had been leaning on it, on top of her.

They tangled together helplessly, their hands, arms, and legs struggling wildly to become free of the other person's limbs.

He suddenly became aware that one of her breasts was under his left hand. It was firm and soft. He felt his face slowly starting to burn as he realized that he was touching naked flesh—not clothing!

He hurriedly removed his hand, and to his horror found himself placing it on her stomach. He struggled and his fingers worked wildly on the sacred portions below.

His face flooded violent red.

Everything was happening too fast for him.

First a near accident.

Then this girl looking at him.

And now this suddenly accidental making passes at her private property.

It was just too much.

He madly wormed himself away from her.

He didn't know what to do or say.

Finally he mumbled: "Gosh, I'm sorry I didn't mean to be fresh." He looked up at her and saw that she was smiling at him.

His stomach began to shake. And suddenly he found himself laughing.

She returned his laughter.

After while when he had gained control of himself, he looked across at her.

They were both sitting on the edge of the road. They were only feet apart.

His eyes bugged as he examined her.

She was the most beautiful girl he had ever seen.

Sexy might be a better word.

Her breast measurements were...*outstanding.*

And he should know; he'd been measuring enough of them the past few weeks.

He blinked several times as he looked at the huge gap at her chest that so revealingly showed the end of one of her nipples. He gulped, not knowing what to do.

He couldn't get his eyes away from the exposed part of her anatomy. They were frozen there. The three top buttons of her shirt must have broken off while the two of them had been trying to unscramble themselves.

He forced his eyes to pull away from her exposed breasts after a long, embarrassed but stimulating moment; but they didn't leave her figure. He followed the lines of her curving body. Her narrow waist, rounded hips, flat stomach, full thighs, long exciting legs , then back to her breasts.

He was fascinated.

He'd sacrifice one hell of a lot to start giving them the once-over with his hands, instead of his eyes

He shook his head and looked up at her face.

She was staring innocently at him.

She must have noticed the direction of his eyes the moment before. But she wasn't doing anything about covering herself up.

She was either dumb and didn't realize or one hell of a sexy doll.

He was afraid it was the former.

Her eyes were amazingly innocent looking.

A damn stupid country girl!

He felt hot all over.

She was just about the sexiest thing he had seen for a long time.

He'd give one hell of a lot to explore ever curve of her lovely figure.

He shook his head and looked away from her.

He wasn't about to get mixed up in a shotgun wedding.

"You okay?" she asked, smiling a bit too invitingly.

"I don't think the car's hurt...just my nerves." He tried hard to think of something to say.

He couldn't think of anything interesting or important.

Finally, he blurted out: "By the way, my name's Henry Forrest...selling my way across the states."

"Mine's Sally," she exclaimed suddenly. "What do you sell?"

"Oh I...ah..." His eyes paralyzed themselves to her breasts. He tried hard to pull them away, but he didn't have what it took to do so. "I sell well women's *things*." His voice cracked high pitched as he spoke the last words.

"What kind of women's *things?*" she asked, her voice light and innocent.

You know damn well! Or at least guess!

He could see in her eyes she was well aware of what he was trying to say; and amused at his embarrassment.

"Well you know...just things." His voice cracked again.

What was wrong with him? This was his business. He talked to women about his products every day

In a fury of action she removed her shirt, exposing herself completely.

His eyes banged in their sockets.

His heart almost burst inside him.

His stomach turned upside down.

Gee, what did she think she was doing?

"You have something for these?" Her voice sounded airy, and completely unaware of how daring she was being.

But he wondered if it wasn't just an act.

He had plenty of things for her products on display, but he was just afraid to show them for they might not be what she was after.

One couldn't take any chances with these country girls.

He felt sick. His body was burning horribly. It wouldn't take much to get him to move over to her and make the hell out of that lush, delightful body.

If we were in the city, I'd know damn well what you wanted...and you'd get it for sure.

But...

He looked away and coughed nervously. With an effort he made his voice sound professional.

"Well, I believe I could get what you want...I ah...would have to order *them* for you." He stood nervously. "I'll have to get my order book and measuring tape..."

He stumbled awkwardly toward the car.

It took him some time to find his order book. It was under the front seat. Then he got the tape measure from the glove compartment.

When he turned around, Sally wasn't there.

Where had she gone?

Run out on him?

"Sally? Where are you?" he called out.

"I'm over here!" her voice answered from behind the large oak tree.

"What are you doing there?" he asked, a little surprised.

"You'll find out," she laughed.

He moved around the tree and came to a sudden stop.

Lying on the ground, hidden from the road, she looked up at him.

She had *nothing* on.

His heart bounced. His face flushed. His muscles shivered nervously, and excited.

"I want you to fill another order for panties," she smiled, looking up at him. Her mouth opened slightly, and her tongue worked delicately between her parted teeth.

This time he knew just what she was after.

He hungrily lay down beside her and took her slightly shivering body in his arms. He felt trembling arms slide around his neck as her mouth touched his. Her lips were velvety and warm. They seemed to be shaky as they moved open under his. Her tongue worked savagely between her parting teeth. Her body clutched hard to his. She kissed him with everything she had and that was one hell of a lot. An excited ripple ran convulsively through her.

He moved his hand down to her breast. It felt firm and soft to his touch. It pressed up hard against his hand. Her teeth ground lightly at his ear. Her fingers gripped nervously at his hair, pulling and clawing.

Boy, she's so sexed up she can't wait!

Her lips spread on his neck, and he felt the warm moisture of her tongue working between them.

These country girls...real sex pots.

Her hands were starting to pull aside his shirt, and finally she pulled herself against his naked flesh.

Fire spurted through him. His nerves grew raw with passion. His body ached with it. She caressed him. She pulled

70

the rest of his clothing from him, and gave her body to his.

Afterwards she clawed at him again. Hungrily. Passionately.

Her tongue worked frantically behind her lips, and she crushed them to his. Her body started working against him again until he could stand it no longer. He returned her hunger.

He satisfied her desires and she demanded more.

Her hunger only matched his own and it was turning dark before either were finished or tired.

* * * * * * *

It was very late when Sally Bankes returned to her uncle's farmhouse. But she felt good at last. She was satisfied for the first time since she had come to the country.

It'd been a real profitable afternoon after all.

She'd gotten more than she could ever have dreamed possible.

And no one would talk because no one would be around who knew except herself and she didn't talk about such matters.

And to top it all off, she had on a new pair of panties and a soft feeling bra, free samples he'd given her!

Yes, she laughed happily to herself. If any more salesmen came around like that one she just *might* find the country not such a bad place after all...*not a bad place at all.*

ಬFITTE THE THIRTEENTHಲ

And here's another "hot little number" considering its open-ing statement. And one does have to believe what they read, after all. A variation of the previous story, immediately quite obvious! Yet with its differences.

*SUDDENLY LUST SUMMER*ಲ

It was terribly hot. A heat that broke down from the skies and cracked and dried everything it touched. It squeezed the body into a tired, restless, desiring thing.

That's the way summer affected Ruth Carlton. It burned her insides to cinders. Her skin crawled in tingling pains. Her muscles felt shaky and even the marrow of her bone seemed to give a heated quiver.

She hated the heat. She hated summer. Summer brought the pain, the agony, and the hurt.

She couldn't keep her hands off her body. The nerves were raw. They felt cruelly grated. And breathing was so blasted hard. It was a terrible effort that racked her lungs, and expanded her chest, and bobbed the large balls of flesh that danced searchingly there.

But there were no caressing hands, and seeking fingers, no hungry lips.

She shivered convulsively.

Something had to happen. Something had to be done. She needed a man, like ham needed eggs, like cars needed roads, like engines needed gas, like fire needed air.

Quickly she dressed.

FLUFF, BY CHARLES NUETZEL

She'd get herself a man; she'd get herself a man!

* * * * * * *

Ben Winters liked the hot summer sun. It worked over his body with soothing fingers, pushing oiling sweat from the anxious glands, burning the surface skin to dark brown.

It was a man's life.

And what a life it was, Ben was on his vacation. And that was a laugh! Vacation from what?

Wine, women and song!

But then, there was nothing like the life of a rich lover. And he lived it up to the fullest.

Women found him all they desired in a man. The corny term tall, dark and handsome fit perfectly. It had been created for him. At least if that wasn't true, it should be.

Yet, there was a time for everything. And now was a time to rest. Vacation time, in sunny California. It was a relief to be away from grasping, sex-starved females.

Not that he didn't like them. He loved them; literally!

The trouble with women was that they wanted so much out of him. Money, jewels, apartments, dresses, and then they started trying to get with the serious stuff! And that he just couldn't take.

He had just run from one marriage-minded sexy little woman in New York. Now he was on an extended vacation, at a lonely stretch of beach, staying in the summer home of a friend of his, Brad Rayberry.

It was a good place. A wonderfully stocked bar. Three bedrooms, living room, play room, and den, with the normal ultra modern convenient fixtures.

What a life!

"Excuse me," a silky, low-pitched, feminine voice interrupted his thoughts.

He opened his eyes.

Blue sky. Nothing else.

Was lie dreaming?

"Pardon me?" the voice repeated itself. It came before from behind him.

He turned and looked.

Such a lovely creature! Such a delight to the eyes.

He recoiled violently.

What was wrong with him? Women were the last things he wanted to get involved with.

He was on a vacation!

"What's wrong?" she smiled, her lips making a sexy twist as they curled up into that delightful, humorous expression.

What a woman!

His eyes could not be stopped from running along the curving lines of her figure. Such hips. Such narrow waist. Such beautiful swells of chest material. Such a revealing bathing suit. She really had it!

She dipped down beside him, and he couldn't help noticing the luscious crevice between her mountains.

She sighed and trembled slightly.

It shocked him.

He had planned to surprise her. To scare her off. Instead she had come to him with a desperate eagerness; a longing passion.

With a jolting abruptness he jerked away from her.

Rising, he walked toward the house several yards away. Up the steps. Opened the door. Into the living room. Over to the bar. Quickly mixed himself a martini. Drank it down in one gulp.

It hit his stomach. Painfully. Shot through his blood, nerves, muscles, bone, and brain. Numbed him. He mixed another, drank it down in one gulp. Reacted.

What was happening to the world. Women just didn't come up to strange men and start acting like she had. And not such beautiful women. No questions asked. No answers given. No such woman could exist in reality.

Of course she just wasn't! He had made her up out of his mind.

He had always been looking for the free, sex-starved creature who would come out and offer herself without charge, without strings attached. Without desiring anything except the enjoyment of a loving mate.

But this was just too fantastic to be real.

Downing another drink he moved to the curtained window, pulled aside the shades and looked out across the beach.

She was lying out in the sand.

He blinked.

Shocked.

She had pulled off her bathing suit.

She was lying there, bathing in the hot summer sun, without a thing on.

He had never seen such a body. Such a delight. Such wonderful curves and swells.

Suddenly he didn't care if she was a dream or not. He didn't care what it would cost him. He forgot he was on a vacation. He forgot everything except the burning ache in his guts that cried to take her, to walk out there on the sand and reach down and enfold that lovely body in his arms.

Maybe it was the drink. Maybe it was the passion.

He didn't care. He didn't care at all!

He walked out of the room, out of the house, onto the sand, and over to where that naked Goddess waited. There were no words. None were needed. They both desired the other. They both knew what was expected. They both took and gave what was necessary.

* * * * * * *

Ruth Carlton walked into the New York office of Brad Rayberry, smiling thankfully. She plopped down on the large leather chair that faced the long modern desk.

"Well, Brad, you were right!" she announced happily.

"I told you...knowing Benny," the heavy set, elderly business tycoon explained.

"Sure thing...thanks for tipping me in on where he was staying. If there ever was a man like him, I never found him. He seemed even grateful for the affair. Grateful that I came, without word, questions, or requests!" she grinned from ear to ear. "What a summer vacation! What a vacation. I don't know what I would have done if you hadn't cued me in on Ben. We really made out."

Brad smiled knowingly. "When you were making such desperate attempts to get men, and I knew just what you

75

were looking for, it didn't take long to lead you in the right direction."

"And the pay off..." she exclaimed in excitement. "He wants us to meet next summer... Won't it be delightful?...free love!"

℘FITTE THE FOURTEENTH℘

Well, there are many ways to a woman's heart, and to the lusting passions of her body, no matter how cool, even cold, she might appear in the beginning. The trick was discovering what turned her on. In this case, it had to do with some very special rites. And he was about to discover the key to…

THE PASSIONATE PAGAN℘

The woman's naked body jerked and shook violently, following the rhythm of the pounding drum beats. She raised her head savagely to the full moon, and her mouth opened, rasping out a horrible passionate scream.

Bill Carter couldn't believe this was the cold, unapproachable Laura La Voie, of *McMeans, Larson & Willers, Insurance.*

It was hard to believe this could be the icy woman no one dared approach. For one look at her cat green eyes, and no man dared attempt to discover the secrets which were always hidden behind the man tailored business suit she always wore to work.

It covered her body; but, not its shape.

Her figure was long and animal like, and moved with a grace that turned a man's guts into pounding pain inside him.

Her breasts were firm pointed bulges, her waist, thin and narrow. Her hips were rounded flares that slid downwards, into perfect thighs. When she walked, the lower torso of her body swung with a gentle sway that caught and held all male eyes.

Her ankles were delicate, her calves excitingly smooth, and shapely, and she kept her black hair knotted in a huge bun, upon the top of her head.

Her face was long and narrow, with high cheek bones; full lips, red and velvety that seemed to demand a man to desire them.

All desired her.

Her eyes told the cold story, exposed the freezing chill of her insides; they looked outwards upon the world, and gave no indication that they were aware of the warmth of human desires, passions, or loves.

She was a sexual animal that refused to indulge in the pleasures of the flesh. She turned down even the warmth of friendship, only showing warmth to Joe Willers, her boss, and the man who had brought her into the organization. But he was as cold as she; or appeared so to the casual onlooker.

Yet Bill Carter couldn't get it out of his mind that under that outer layer of ice, she was a burning volcano, and that she knew the fire of passion, sex, and love. But that icy shell never broke, never cracked, never allowed a peek into the inner core of fire that he felt sure must be there.

But it wasn't the cold shell about her that kept hungry males away. It was the look, and the sharp red nails on the *ends* of her long fingers. Nobody dared a scraping of those claws that she would not fail to use upon the first person foolish enough to touch her.

From the moment he saw her, he wanted her. It was like a sickness that twisted his insides; and it hurt day and night.

"That La Voie girl," he said to a friend of his, one day at lunch. "You know, the one that works for Willers."

"Don't touch her, mister!" his friend offered with alarm. "Don't touch her; she'll cut you to pieces, then throw the parts in the air just to see where they fly."

"I *know!* I'm not about to get caught in such a trap; but, I'd give one hell of a lot to dig past that reserve!"

"You do, and you might be sorry. His friend leaned forward slightly, then whispered softly, as if afraid someone else might hear. "I've heard she belongs to some cult...or something."

Bill felt a smile spread his lips. "Oh, come on...who's

kidding who?"

"No, really, ask Willers...I bet he knows something."

That had ended the conversation, except for a few normal male remarks to the effect that they both would like to have a little fun with this woman.

But it didn't end Bill's hunger; nor his interest.

The next time he was in Willers office, he asked the man about Laura La Voie.

"What's there to know?" the man asked coldly.

"Hell, Joe she works for you...and you gave her the job...some say you knew her before..."

"What business is it of yours?" Willers' eyes looked frigidly up at his.

He felt lost for words. The man seemed insulted. *Hell, why should he be?* "I was just wondering about her. I'd like to get to know her...you know?"

Willers leaned back in his chair, and a strange smile worked over his face. He seemed suddenly lost in another world. "Fiery wench real lover girl!"

His eyes grew dreamy.

"But..." He sat up and looked meaningfully at Bill. "But you got to get her at the right moment."

"When's that?" Excitement moved over him to such a degree, that he felt sick from the effects.

"Just once a month when the moon is full, at midnight." The man's voice trailed off, and a smile spread over his face again. *"The Pagan Rites of the Fire Goddess of Love!"*

Bill didn't know if he was being kidded or...

The man did seem...well...serious...lost in a world outside of the real one.

"Come on, now! That stuff went out in the Dark Ages."

"Not for some; not for those that believe in the exciting ecstasy of love...passion...delights of the flesh that have been handed down only to the sex worshipers...handed down from pagan gods!" His voice was becoming feverous, high pitched. His eyes were glassy.

He suddenly shook his head, and as if coming out of a dream; he wiped his forehead. His eyes slowly dulled, and his face appeared as if he were still dazed. He looked at Bill.

"I didn't mean I mean to imply...well..." Red covered

his features.

"Tell me more," Bill encouraged, not caring now if it were just a fantastic gag or...

It was fantastic! Pagan gods rites held in the light of a full moon!

In the twentieth century?

"There's not much to tell; but to experience, oh, that is something else!"

"You mean you've seen one of these meetings?"

Willers sat up proudly, his shoulders moving back, and his chest pushing forward. "Seen? Man, *I'm one of them!*" His voice broke off as if he had said too much.

"Gosh, I'd sure like to see one of these..." Bill's voice whispered softly, eagerly, excited. He was a little shocked by his own words. He had no idea of what he was getting himself into; but, he didn't care; he had to find out if Laura La Voie was all a man could imagine her to be.

"You wish to come to one of our meetings?" Willers voice was suddenly intense, even excited. "*You* are interested in our pagan gods, our rites?"

"Yes, yes, of course. I'm more than interested. Please...can you, will you? I'd be delighted!"

"Are you sure? There can be danger there for the wrong person. Or, at least, shock. These rites are not for little children, but for burly men and passionate women who are willing to explore the very depths of feelings so totally deep and powerful that it can be a real killer! Be warned!"

"Oh, I'm not afraid."

"Afraid? Terrorized is a better word. If you don't fit it can be damaging to your very soul!" Willers warned.

He didn't even hesitated, for demons and pagan gods and supernatural rites were all foolishness—so if they wanted to play out some fancy game he was game to play it out with them. If it got the woman of his dreams in his arms at last!

"I not at all concerned. I'd be delighted."

The man studied him for a long silent moment, then a slow grin spread across his features.

Willers stood, and shot out his hand toward Bill. "Then it's settled. You'll come with us...you'll see the rites you'll

80

experience the true meaning of passion love...lust!"

The event was several weeks off, and Bill counted the days in anxious excitement. Years passed in those few days.

Every time he saw Laura La Voie during this period, chills of excitement went through him. He would lay awake at nights, imagining the delights of exploring her body; making love to her. It was all he could think of.

Finally the week came, the time of the full moon.

"You are especially honored," Willers said, as they drove along the lonely mountain road, which lead to the secret meeting place of the Worshippers of the Fire Goddess of Love. "It is seldom that the full moon comes on a weekend...And it is only at such times that we are able to continue our worship for two nights and two days...and endless feast of passions you have never witnessed before in your life. Assuming, of course, you pass all the ritual tests and come out with sparkling colors!"

"I'm not afraid," he assured the man, finding it difficult to keep from laughing in his face. Such childish, silly, warning were down right hysterical. You'd think they were talking about some demon from hell.

It was late when they arrived at their destination; a mountain top, hidden at the end of a little known road on the top of the world. Or at least that's what the sign had said: "Turn right for the Top of the World!"

There was a huge stone building, and a large clearing surrounding it, in which were parked hundreds of cars. People were milling around, talking, laughing, and exchanging news. They looked normal; like a church group about to attend a social gathering: not members of a strange, weird pagan cult!

"I told Laura about you and your interest in our rites...she seemed pleased." Willers said, as they started toward the gigantic building. He turned and smiled.

"I think she's interested in you..." he winked.

"Well, she *is* one of the reasons..."

"I know and she was flattered."

There were three entrances into the large pagan temple, and Willers pointed to one saying: "You go through that door, and you'll be given a change in clothing, and a place to put your civvies. Then go out the far door in the dressing room to the inner temple. Don't speak to anyone; for it is against all the rules of the creed. No one talks until the spoken rites have been said, and the worship has begun. If you break that rule, you'll be kicked out, forever!"

"Where are you going?" Bill asked, surprised and a little worried at being left to his own devices. He had hoped that Willers would be at his side to instruct him.

"I have duties and a part to play...you'll see!" A weird light entered the man's dark eyes as he spoke then he smiled, and patting Bill on the shoulder, he turned and walked toward the middle entrance.

After he had disappeared, Bill moved toward the door he had been told to use. He was nervous. His stomach was grinding. His head felt dizzy. He almost wished he hadn't come.

Pagan rights could get out of hand

Inside, he found himself facing an old gnarled man, wearing nothing but a plain G-string. The man smiled, and said: "Greetings, oh fellow worshipper, take these gifts," he extended a G-string like the one he wore, "and dress in the ways of the gods."

Bill took the offering and walked over to where the man indicated.

He changed into the narrow G-string, placed his clothing in the locker before him, and then walked out the door at the far end of the room.

He felt ridiculous. Regardless of the possible offerings, he wondered if it was going to be worth all the trouble and long, anxious, waiting days. He had never felt so silly.

And these people actually believed all that silly crap about whatever they believed in. Whatever that might be.

Suddenly he began wondering if there might be more to this than he'd suspected.

As he stepped through the door, and looked beyond, he was shocked to a standstill.

He had no idea so many people would be here.

He found himself in a huge outdoor "arena" type theater, or temple. He decided temple was a better word. In the center of the round arena was a gigantic disk of huge stone slabs, a huge black pit in its center. Around the pit were large metal urns, fires burning in them.

Straw mats covered the ground from the edge of the disk, to the outer, enclosing walls, and along the walls were huge drums of all shapes. Several people already were gathered at the edge of the disk.

He was scared, not knowing what to expect, or what was expected of him. He wanted to run, but it was too late.

A shudder ran through him, but he forced his feet forward, to stop at the edge of the disk, where he sat down between two women.

One of the women was old and monstrously fat; the other was thin and young, breasts hidden on her chest, skin stretched tightly across her bones.

Both acted as if they didn't even notice his arrival. Their eyes were centered on the disk, while their breaths were heavy pants that shook their bodies.

He crossed his legs under him, and stared forward like the others.

He found it hard to keep his eyes from jumping from one person to the other, as they seated themselves around the other side of the disk. They all seemed in a trance.

Some were beautiful. Others were old and fat, or shriveled.

When the arena was almost full, huge traps opened suddenly from the black pit, and completely naked men ran out, forced their way through the crowded people, almost knocking some over in their passage, and came to a stop along the walls. When there was a complete circle of them, they picked up huge mallets, and as if controlled by one mind, they all started beating the drums. The roar pounded at Bill's ears, deafening them in its thunder. He wanted to cover his ears, but didn't dare for fear of insulting those surrounding him.

Then, without warning, the disk filled with beautiful young maidens clothed in filmy gowns. They started dancing to the drum beats, their bodies swaying and jerking gently with the rhythmic savage pounding. Their heads rolled on their shoulders, long hair flying from left to right.

It was....

Fantastic.

Sexual.

Exciting.

Then they came to an abrupt halt and the drums went silent.

From out of the pit stepped a man, clothed in gold, jewels and silks. He wore a headpiece of solid diamonds. Bill never had seen anything like it, not even in the movies.

The young dancing girls sat in a circle around the man; their arms reaching towards his face

He raised his head toward the full moon. "Hear ye, oh worshipers of the Goddess of Love, The Cult of the Most Sacred Passions...strip your minds of all thoughts, all wishes, all dreams, and know only the truth of which I speak!"

The voice sounded slightly familiar. Then with a mental jolt, Bill realized the shocking truth. He couldn't believe his eyes.

Joe Willers!

"Oh, God of Love...Fire Goddess of all delight and pleasures...burn through my body...caress it with a flame that fires every cell, every nerve...char my brain to black vigor...possess my body, and show me all the joys that are yours to give..." His voice had reached a fever pitch the drums started to beat slowly, and the maidens started swaying their bodies from left to right, matching the rhythm of the drums.

Then out of the pit leaped the most beautiful woman that Bill's eyes ever had fallen upon.

No sooner had she escaped the pit, than it went up in flame, a huge fire bursting forth and lighting the temple as if it were day. A moan went through the audience, to grow pulsating with the drums, adding music to their meter.

The woman was dressed only in gold breast plates, and silk G-string. She had long black hair that swung as she moved her head. Her body jerked from left to right accenting the beat of the drummers. She opened her mouth in a wild scream, savage in volume.

Her arms moved madly in the air, her hips twisted and jumped with the writhing of her body. Her breasts danced as she quivered and shook.

She danced as if possessed by a fiery devil of passion.

A pagan woman of the Pagan God of Love.

Suddenly her breasts plates flew unlatched, exposing huge mountains of soft velvet flesh, bouncing, swinging, rolling, and jerking.

With a shock that jogged his brain to numbness, he recognized her cold green eyes, now lighted to deep emerald in the fire; her long curving body.

Laura La Voie!

She was in a daze of pagan excitement, a burning, human animal that demanded to be made love to.

All around him people were standing, jerking, and swaying, and dancing to the drums that heat faster and faster, louder amid louder.

Everyone was in a fever pitch, going wildly insane.

At a fever pitch, everybody was beginning to claw at each other, beginning their rites. Even the dancing maidens were moving from the stone dusk, to pair off with male partners.

Now as the time!

He looked up at the disk, seeking out the pagan woman La Voie.

She was dancing in the middle of the disk, near the fire pit. jerking, twisting in mad, insane fashion. Her body would bend downwards, her head falling between her legs, then she snapped upright, arms reaching for the sky, screaming wildly at the full moon, her figure shaking sporadically. An old shriveled man jumped onto the disk, running toward her. He grabbed her body, and it incited violently against his. Her arms wrapped around him and her mouth sought his in a wild hungry fashion that made Bill's mind go red with rage.

Nobody was going to take her away from him!

He leaped to the disk, toward the woman he desired, and the man trying to take her away with him.

With all the strength he possessed, he tore the horrid creature from Laura La Voie. The woman didn't even notice; she just started dancing wildly. The man was completely unaware of what had happened; he ran from the disk toward another woman.

Bill turned and faced the squirming, jerking form of La

Voie. She was in a blind trance, unaware of what was happening.

Then recognition seeped into her eyes, and she smiled; a twisted curl of her lips. She moved toward him. Her body pressed next to his, and her arms slid around his neck, her fingers caressing, softly demanding; tenderly encouraging; then passionately grabbing.

Her breasts crushed hard and soft against his chest; her hips rammed against his; as her body begged to be taken. Her lips shoved to his, soft, warm, open. Her tongue moved eagerly.

He took her.

He held her to him with all the violence, all the desperate agony built up in for all these months since he had first seen her.

He caressed the delightful excitement of her body, and she returned his fiery touch with her own hands.

They locked together, their bodies becoming one heated fusion.

They enjoyed the thrilling exchange of passion, lust, and love for two nights and two days, living on the diet of their excited ecstasy.

The next Monday at work, Bill Carter expected to find Laura La Voie friendlier, more aware of his existence, and show some sign that she still desired him, as much as he desired her.

But the cold green ice had returned to her eyes; the hard indestructible shell was back in place.

She did not even know he existed.

He was a stranger.

But he shrugged inwardly. He could wait. He could wait until the moon was full. Then things would be different, and he would again experience the most thrilling excitement that any woman was capable of giving

Yes, he smiled to himself, *he could wait...*

86

✂FITTE THE FIFTEENTH✂

Now, come along and tell me the truth, wouldn't you go for this kind of experience, this kind of meeting? Isn't this the ideal fantasy? If this be fluff, then consider how nice it could be to find a lovely woman on a beach, with whom to share something very special. And our hero here found such a beautiful...

NUDE ON A LONELY BEACH✂

Coming upon a naked girl lying on the beach can be a surprising and shocking thing.

Coming upon the most beautiful woman you have ever seen in such a condition is something more: it is excitingly overpowering.

And William Rarsons could hardly believe his *eyes.* It made him dizzy, as he looked down at the lovely creature, whose curving figure, and large well formed, pointed breasts, exposed themselves completely to his astonished eyes.

She was asleep, unaware of him.

He should probably leave quietly.

But he couldn't move. He found himself *wanting* her to know he was there.

He wanted to draw her full supple body to him, stroking it, fondling it, caressing it, kissing and making love to it.

He should slip away before she discovered him.

Instead he stood like a statue, paralyzed to the floor of the beach; frozen to stone, by the beautiful sight of this sea goddess.

Her soft lips, her long curled blonde hair, her narrow waist, flat stomach, rounded hips, long well formed thighs and legs held him in a magnificent spell of desire.

And the loneliness inside him, the ache for woman's love, passion, her body and soul fairly drown him in lingering hunger.

It was a lonely beach, the shoreline untouched by civilized hands. Farms, houses only dotted the lands on the other side of the quiet road; the highway of mankind. But all that *was* somewhere else, in another world.

He felt as a man suspended in a timeless dimension where anything might happen; where a sea Goddess might appear on the sandy beach, naked and beautiful, to tempt him into the ocean depths or into a fiery passion of ecstasy.

It was a hot day, and he had bean driving for hours without rest. Suddenly he had seen the cool soothing beauty of the ocean and the urge built in him to rest; swim; feel the soft giving grains of sand moving between his toes.

And he had been drawn to the shore and this beautiful temptress..

He was nuts!

He couldn't get his eyes off the full, points of her breasts, large peaks, rising and falling on her chest, as she breathed. He wanted to caress them, touch their silky smoothness; he wanted to make love to her, take her body to his and...

Rape her?!... Hardly! *But no one would ever know!*

What was wrong with him?

He had never thought such ideas before, but then, he had never come across a naked woman in such an isolated spot. What was she doing there? Did she feel it was totally safe to sunbath nude?

Was she a nudist? Or a goddess? Or what?

He suddenly found himself wanting to know about her...what she was doing here all by herself...What *was* she like?

He wanted to know: Everything.

But most of all he wanted to possess her; it was as if he were in a spell; a total trance

Must be the sun.... Maybe she didn't really even ex-

ist...was an illusion.

The sun.

He looked at the sun. It was blinding bright. He looked back at the girl.

She wasn't there!

He blinked, feeling sick

Then slowly she reappeared, as the sun blindness seeped away.

He knelt beside her, and his hands reached out. He couldn't stop them. Only one thought seem to motivate him: he had to feel; he had to know for sure that she was actually real, not some strange image created out of an exhausted mind.

Carefully his fingers sought contact, touched the soft, velvety flesh of her arm.

It shocked him!

He withdrew his hand violently...

...*afraid!*

He hadn't really expected to feel anything but empty air. Maybe.

But she was there!

He sat dumbly, as she stirred, then abruptly opened her eyes.

They were large, and deep blue. They had a hidden beauty far greater than the outer perfection of her sexual body! Almost misty, cloudy.

Then a darkness came over them; anger. An ugly monster, had taken possession of her. Her face flushed with shame, horror, fear. Terror moved her features one after another; then the redness of embarrassment took final control. She reacted quickly, trying to cover herself up.

She turned her back to him, lying on her stomach, in an effort to conceal herself. It was no use, and after a moment she seemed to realize it.

She looked up, disgust moved her facial muscles. "What kind of man are you?"

Her voice held horrid contempt, each word clipped and harsh.

He didn't know what to say.

He was just a normal male, who suddenly had found

himself hypnotized by a beautiful naked woman, who seemed to have appeared from nowhere, stretched on her back, in the white sand. He just looked at her helplessly, red covering his face.

Her eyes moved from his face, following the lines of his broad shoulders, large, well formed arms and chest; down to his toes. They held icy coldness during their entire journey. Then they popped back to his face and eyes, boring inwards, like knives, trying to cut away the wall which covered his inner being

"I didn't mean to be...well...I was driving along the road...and it was a hot day...and well...how the hell was I to know an outlandishly beautiful nude woman was sunbathing on the shore?"

He felt sudden anger. It hadn't been his fault. Why should he feel like a degenerate?

"Hell, I couldn't help looking. I'm just normal, and damn it all, I didn't put you here."

Her eyes had a questioning look, as if she were trying to understand his viewpoint and was having difficulty. Finally the corners of her lips smiled slightly.

"I guess, well, I," she stammered hesitantly. "I probably shouldn't have come out in the raw...but this beach is so lonely, and I haven't seen anybody on it for months...I live only across the road...I thought I'd be perfectly safe and well...

"Please turn around don't look at me...it makes me...feel...well...naked. Please?" trying to hide herself.

He looked at the ocean, the horizon, at the sky with its sea-gulls dancing back and forth in their clear sea of air and down at the sand and the rolling waves that moved back and forth, in and out like desperate watery arms.

They were alone, on a hidden beach: a man...and a woman.

He wanted her desperately. He needed her!

It was like he had been put on a desert, without water or food for an eternity, then, with no warning at all, discovered himself transplanted into a land of plenty.

His hunger burst into uncontrolled flame.

No, *more* than hunger. Desire, passion, and, strangely

90

enough deep tenderness.

And he saw those same emotions reflected in her misty eyes; she was like him. Alone, hungry for the food and drink of desire.

"This is silly," she murmured in a husky voice, very near him.

He knew what she meant. "I know, and we're strangers."

Her face flushed, her eyes brightened with excitement. Her breath became heavy.

"No, *no!*" she cried, brokenly, hardly above a whisper. "We can't, we shouldn't...I shouldn't think such thoughts..." A tremor ran through her body. "No not now...not now!"

"It's the sun," he said, trying to give her a way out of the struggling, desperate emotional desires.

"I...I don't know." She was still short of breath. "I've never felt this way before. It's silly...I don't even know you...yet, I *do*..."

"Funny, strangers meet under difficult circumstances, and something seems to happen...or develop or something..." His voice trailed into nothingness.

"You could have taken advantage of me any time while we have been here alone...you didn't!" Her face was very near his. It would be easy to lean forward slightly, kiss her.

"It's as if I've been waiting for you to come along. I somehow know you're kind, gentle, considerate, tender...I can see that in your eyes...when another might have...done something...you didn't!"

She leaned very close. Her lips almost touching his.

"Kiss me. Please!" Her arms slid around him, pulling her close against his body. She felt warm; exciting; soft; delicate; passionate

He held her close, returning her kiss with tender warmth, a desperate hunger. Then gently he laid her down on the sand. Leaning over her, he looked deep into her eyes. He silently questioned.

Her lips whispered softly, "Be gentle..." and he knew more about her from those two words than he ever had known about any other person.

He took her in his arms, and slowly made love to her.

He searched her body with his hands, fingers, lips caressing, softly seducing, and finally passionately, in a heat of desperate desire, making violent love to her, which she returned with the same burning explosive fashion.

Their bodies burned and they crushed savagely to each other, they clawed cruelly and wildly.

He had wanted to be gentle; she had wanted him to be. Instead they both mutually ravished one another like starving beasts. They could not control the horrible ache that took possession of their minds and bodies.

It was pure animal, hurting, volcanic. It was as if lava had been poured over their nerves, burning them to cinders; and it would not stop

"I've never done anything like this before," she breathed softly, lips hardly moving.

"I know I know."

"I never...never had a man...I mean, this is so wonderful!"

He wanted her again. Now and later; much later. He wanted to learn her likes and dislikes. He wanted to be told about her childhood, about her loves and hates; he wanted to become a part of her world.

Tenderly he kissed her. He wanted to tell her how beautiful she was, to express in words how he felt, but he couldn't.

Instead he held her close, kissing her lips, her cheeks, her neck, her shoulders; then he looked deep into her eyes. He knew she felt the same; wanted him to be near her like this...his for the taking. .

She was his. His alone. At this moment nobody but the two of them existed and neither of them cared about anything other than this moment and their mutual sharing. Their mutual mating, bonding, on a lonely beach. With a stranger.

He held her tenderly, and slowly made love to her...

It was like a dream, a fantasy, which had come true. And at that moment he had no idea of its reality, nor if it would last beyond this one special afternoon. Perhaps that might be enough for both of them.

Perhaps this was only the beginning.

℘FITTE THE SIXTEENTH℘

A sad little tale, I must admit. It was published a number of times, and I'll never know why, exactly. Not that it isn't "fluffy" enough, just that it is a harsh reminder of what some women find themselves facing when they runaway and attempt to survive in the Big City.

BIRTH OF A CALL GIRL℘

"A dime for some coffee...a dime for...?" the ragged old man said over and over, as people passed by him on the bleak and dirty street. "A dime for some coffee?"

Nobody paid him any attention, except a young attractive woman, standing on a corner, a winter coat wrapped around her, as if she had nothing else on.

She was quite a looker! he thought, eyeing what was showing of her figure. *Quite a looker.*

But what's she doing here in this part of town? No place for a girl like her—unless she's looking for a pick up.

A man who could get a few minutes with her in bed would be lucky indeed. Even he'd like that; even at his age.

She smiled shyly at him with her wide full mouth. Her eyes were sad, slightly sunken.

She'd been in town—the big city, for five weeks now, and she couldn't return home—not after all that she had said, not after going off with Mr. Harryton, who had promised her large contracts, fame, a wonderful future in the big city! With her talents, he had told her, you'll go places.

Talents—that was a laugh; a bitter laugh!

93

FLUFF, by Charles Nuetzel

They had not been twenty-five miles out of her home town when he pulled up to a small hotel.

"Look, baby," he had said, turning toward her, and looking coldly into her eyes. "If you want to get along in the big city...you'll have to learn a few things...a few pointers...ideas on how to work your way up...how to get started...and make important men willing to give a lot of time and money to advance your career."

He had gotten out of the car then, walked around to her door, opened it, and helped her out.

"We'll stop here for the night." It was early, hardly three, and there was no reason that she could think of to stop now or here.

A little nervous tightness quivered her stomach muscles. But she didn't hesitate, because Mr. Harryton had been nice to her; advised her; and was now willing to teach her the tricks of the trade.

She was afraid of what might be coming, and she didn't know quite how to handle things. Well, she never had had relations with a man before—not in *that* way.

She liked them all right—in fact, she got a little dizzy when she was held in any man's arms. She liked men, sure, but she'd been raised in a small town.

Mr. Harryton had come through on his way to New York, and seen her in the senior play, and after the show had said she had talent. If she wanted to come to the big city after she graduated; he'd take her. It was only a matter of days before she was finished with school, a diploma in her hands, facing a new life.

He had waited those few days, and here they were on their way to the city, stopping off at a motel.

She was a little afraid.

She'd left home for good; or at least until she made a name for herself in show business!

And she was afraid of what was ahead.

But she did like Mr. Harryton a little in a romantic way. He *was* handsome, and had a way about him. Maybe it wouldn't be so bad.

"You wait here, while I make the arrangements," he said, moving toward the small cottage that was the office.

94

She stood by the car for a long time, waiting. It was a hot day, and she was perspiring by the time he returned with the manager.

"This young lady?" the man grinned. "Well, lady, I hope you enjoy your stay here."

That had sounded strange, but she didn't question the matter until they were alone in the small cottage.

"What's the idea?" she demanded, feeling a flush of anger run up her face. It was one thing to try seducing a girl, quite another to be so blunt about it.

"Oh, cut it, Milly. I had to tell him we were married. He didn't have no other rooms, and it didn't matter anyhow."

That's when he had come over to her, and taken her in his arms.

This was it! her mind screamed.

"What are you doing?" she cried, trying to sound disgusted and horrified, but something in her was excited; almost anxious. "Mr. Harryton! Please!"

"Baby, I only want to kiss you a little—you got to learn about how to make a man happy—how…"

She resisted, even cried out in alarm a little; but she realized she wanted him to take her. For the first time in her life, she felt like a woman; a desirable woman—and she liked it.

His caresses on her body were rough and coarse, nothing gentle or kind, and it almost repulsed her at first. But she found herself liking the crude sensations—the delightful, thrilling touch; the electric feel.

"That's the baby, that's the baby," he whispered in her ear, caressing her breasts, pushing his mouth down on hers again, open and moist. "I knew you'd like it—"

She wrapped her arms around his neck, and pulled him closer; wanting to be taken: wanting to be seduced.

It had been the first time; and she was surprised how much she liked it; how thrilling it had been; how wonderful!

They lay on the bed for a long time afterwards. Then he sat up, looking down at her.

"See, baby see, it was all right. It was nice, wasn't it?" he whispered huskily.

"Yes oh, yes…I never dreamed…my body's still burning—still fiery…still excited." He broke out in a laugh, a nasty, amused laugh. "You want more...baby...you want more!" He moved closer to her, taking her in his arms. "Why, you're burning up...you really like it...don't you?"

"Oh, yes, kiss me. Make love—make me." She hungrily crushed closer and sought his body with a terrible ache; with a terrible demanding desire and a fiery passion.

She had never known life could be so thrilling; that anything could be so exciting.

And she found herself growing more anxious, more thrilled, more passionate as they continued. Time and again she wanted him to take her—time and again her body burned like fire.

It was as if a horrible volcano had suddenly exploded inside her, and it was a terrible pain; a terrible thing that got worse, and worse.

As she stood on the street corner, watching the old man begging for dimes, she realized how close she had been that night to begging, pleading for more caresses, more loving— and she remembered with a terrible, burning pain, how he had taught her all the exciting things, the thrilling actions, which could be enjoyed by man and woman.

They had stayed at the motel for almost a week, thrilling in the excitement of each other's bodies; then they had come to the city.

She bitterly shivered. Her eyes watered. She felt shame.

He had suggested the horrid business of selling her body to men.

"Baby, with your talents, you can make more money than either of us could ever know what to do with."

"Oh. God what kind of person do you think I am?" she had cried.

"Look, I taught you the whole works. You're an expert! You'd make any mark happy...what difference does it make?"

"It was different with you..." she had tried to explain. When he couldn't understand she had walked out, throwing on a coat to cover her nakedness.

Now she wished she hadn't been so quick. He had her clothing, her money, and she wasn't about to go back to get it. She hated him and was afraid of him and *most* of all, she had pride—she wouldn't ever go back to him or anywhere near him, no matter what!

But she had to do something.

She'd thought that maybe she loved him. She had given in to him, because of that deep emotion inside her, until she started enjoying the excitement of his love making; then it had been something out of her control.

She suddenly realized that she was terrible strongly sexed.

God, no!

But deep in her heart she knew that she was over-sexed. She must be. She wanted a man right now—any man!

She needed her body to be caressed and taken, to be made love to over and over, again and again and never to stop.

She knew how wrong it was; oh, how she knew it!

But to have a man…

She was shivering at the thought, her skin was on fire. Her body burned until she felt that she might fall apart.

She was alone now without money—no food, no home.

How could she make a living?

How could she get a man?

She needed both with her whole body, everything in her,. her nerves, her muscles, her skin, her bones and she *had* to have a man—*now!*

She found herself staring at the beggar, with his hands reaching out toward her.

With a sudden shock, she realized she was standing only inches from him. He was asking her for a dime.

As she realized why she had moved those ten yards which had just a moment before been between them it hurt; but she would out grow that—she'd have to!

But for the present, she would have to work her way up from the bottom.

She needed a man, like an alcoholic needled a drink, like a dopey needed a shot.

She had to have one—any one—and she needed someone to get other men for her. Men who would pay!

It would be a start!

"A dime for coffee? A dime for coffee" the beggar said,

grinning with his toothless mouth.

"No money, no money!" she whispered, sick inside, hating herself—but not being able to stop. "But I have something else!"

She opened her coat slightly, so that only he could see her nakedness "Something else for you...you live nearby?"

Her words, her actions, and her painful overpowering desires, sickened her. Yet, maybe it was all that which had moved her away from a comfortable home, a safe place, in a small town which never let a single girl live a really satisfying sexual existence. Maybe all along she had simply wanted men and was afraid to have them under those circumstances.

But she'd rather start with him, than go back to Mr. Harryton; the man responsible—*she still had some pride!*

"Yes, sir, madam!" the wrinkled old face cried eagerly, grabbing hold of her hand, and pulling her along the street.

"Yes—yes..."

It was a point of pure pride! She decided, suddenly at peace with herself. It had to start someplace. And this old man was better than nothing. She was hungry, and needy, and wanted a bed to sleep in. And he would, surely, be easy to control—he would let her stay the night and that's all he really wanted.

She would make it on her own or not at all!

&FITTE THE SEVENTEENTH&

Soul mates are a standard product of romantic fiction. And here we find two people who meet and fall in love. But the price tag is heavy. It is fluff of a different nature.

Beyond that, there's a real story behind this story, or, more correctly, ahead of this story. Let me put it another way: I wrote it, I used some of it in a totally different fashion as part of my first novel, and then later offered this original version to the magazine editor who published it. While the story has little to do with the novel, other than some of the words being used in it, what follows stands alone as a totally different creation. (Writers do, sometimes, cannibalize their stories when needed.) So I offer this version of...

BIG DAVE'S GIRL&

"Open up, Flyboy," a hard, high pitched man's voice cried through the paneling of the door of Barry Larson's clingy hotel room.

Joan hugged closer to him, terror filling her eyes. "Oh, God!" she whispered. "That's Tommy, one of Dave's men. They must have found out—"

"It might just be business...maybe!" But Barry didn't believe his own words. His gut twisted as he stood up, pulling Joan Withers along after him. He pushed her to the side of the door which would hide her once it had been opened. "Quiet!" he hardly whispered into her ear.

"Come on, Flyboy, open up!"

"Just a second." He opened the door.

99

A fist smashed out at him. He staggered backwards. Another fist sank into the pit of his stomach. He doubled over, and a hammer like object fell down on the back of his head. He collapsed to the floor as a scream sounded from the blackness which was flooding over him.

He fought for consciousness. He had to keep awake!

He had to get up! Fight!

He struggled with his muscles. He tried to push his body upwards through the black whirlpool in which he had fallen.

Hands reached down and pulled him upright. They were rough, hard, and cruel.

"Come on, Flyboy, you'll live!" The words were thin and faraway sounding.

The blackness was slowly beginning to lessen.

"Leave him alone, don't hurt him. It wasn't his fault...I came here, he had nothing to do with it..." It was Joan's voice, pleading.

"Shut your damn mouth!" the high pitched male voice rasped. It sounded very close to Barry's ears. "I'll let Big Dave decide what to do about him...and you! Now help me with your flyboy."

He felt soft tender hands take hold of him, as the black clouds around his eyes started to open, letting in light and shape. The room was spinning dizzily, and his stomach and head hurt. He felt himself being seated on the bed.

As things slowly started to settle down, he saw a tall ugly man standing before him, a gun in his hands.

"Now listen, Flyboy!" The leering face distorted, as the gunman moved his mouth. "You make one false move and I'll blast your head in! Got me?"

Barry nodded weakly, trying to appear even groggier than he was.

He could feel Joan's arms around him, supporting his body upright, in a sitting position.

He tried to think.

The other man was standing before the small desk now, where the hotel phone was sitting. Picking it up, he stared at Barry, pointing his gun toward him. After a second he spoke into the receiver, giving a number.

He was calling Big Dave.

100

Barry felt his stomach knot in fear and horror. God knew what would happen next. The gangster was neurotic; insane. The man would kill them both.

He had to do something, quick. If he could get away from this man, and then to the airport, their problems would be over.

He could feel Joan trembling next to him. Out of the corner of his eyes he looked at her. Fear showed on her face. Her lips were quivering; her eyes were moist and frowning. He squeezed her hand affectionately, hoping it would give her *some* courage.

"Let me speak to Dave," Tommy said suddenly. Barry had to do something. But what? The man was too far away to make a sudden rush at.

"Dave, I've found Miss Withers...in the Flyboy's apartment. Yes. Okay. Right...I'll take care of him. Okay, leave him to you. Both of them. Yes, I'll watch them." Hanging up the phone, he turned, his thin loose lips smiling. "Dave don't like it not at all! He's coming right over!"

The man walked across the room toward them.

Just a little closer, and I'll be able to jump you! Barry thought, trying to appear dazed. He let his head hang slightly, and acted as if he were having trouble focusing his eyes.

"Dave's going to take care of you two, but good! He'll fix both of you so this won't happen again. He don't like his best girl stepping out on him. And he's got special plan for you, Flyboy..."

The man was close enough.

Barry tensed and leaped upward. He attacked swiftly and efficiently; with a sureness which only years of practice made possible.

The other man reacted with the same speed as Barry; but he was too late. Barry's fists battered at the other's face, stomach and neck, while his knee rammed up into the gangster's groin. The man crumbled to the floor, moaning. Barry kicked at his head, and then picked up the gun that had fallen from the gunman's hand.

He turned to Joan, taking hold of her arm. "Come on, for God's sake...let's get out of here, fast!"

In seconds they were out of the room, minutes later they were on their way to the airport in the car Barry had rented when he arrived in town a few days earlier.

All the way to the airport Barry could feel a horrible knot of fear make his stomach sick. Their chances of escaping before Big Dave got to them, seemed almost nonexistent. But they had to try. The alternative would he to await death.

He looked at Joan, sitting next to him in the car. She was as beautiful as that first night; only last night?

She had on a red dress, the top of which dipped downwards, revealing the soft fullness of her breasts. Her blonde hair was in loose curls on her forehead. Her lips looked moist and velvety; almost childlike: full and red.

He couldn't help wondering if she still felt the same way he did.

"Scared, Joan?"

"I don't know," she smiled up at him, taking hold of his arm. "It's all happening so fast!"

It seemed strange that one moment he had not known her, and then the next she was the whole world to him. And, maybe now, death!

He had felt a strong impulse of emotion for her, when he first saw her at Big Dave's New Year's party. But he hadn't known she was the small-time hood's special girl; or that she was caught in a trap of fear, terror and hate. He had not realized how far Dave would go to keep her under his thumb; that she could not run away from him, because he would kill her if she did.

Maybe Barry had loved her when he first saw her; but he hadn't realized it until he had found her in his apartment earlier this evening. Attraction was one thing; love another.

She had come into his arms, without a word, clutching him madly; pleadingly.

Barry held her tightly to him.

Their lips met in explosive passion.

His mind became dizzy, but he didn't care.

She was here, in his arms.

He picked her up and moved toward the bed in the corner. She kissed his neck and his cheek as he laid her down,

102

and moved beside her. She clung to him, and he held her tightly in return. Her breasts were soft and full under his touch, as he moved his hand down to them. He could feel her body press closer. Her mouth quivered hungrily to his, seeking, searching, demanding. Her whole body was burning warmly.

He was confused as to why, or how, she had come to his room. But he didn't care for the answers now. She was here. She wanted to be made love to. That's all that mattered.

His mind had been possessed with desire for her the moment he had seen tier; it had been fired cruelly, when she had run out after that first, wildly unexpected, embrace the night before, at Big Dave's party. His guts had been ripped apart by the fact that he had lost her before he even knew her name. And now finding her here, and making love to her, which she returned without excuse, reason, or word, he was not about to try understanding. He could only caress her, kiss her, and return her love in the same violent unembarrassed passion and desire which she had expressed.

His fingers ran along the soft nakedness of her flesh, and it shivered with the excitement of his touch. Her mouth was moist and thrilling. Her breath matched the pounding ache of his own.

The hunger and fervor she explosively demonstrated was not just passion; it was something else too. And he knew he felt the same intangible emotion.

Something had happened when the two of them had met the night before. And that sudden surprising, impulsive kiss had not been a sexual exchange. It had been a mutual need. The need of two lovely people reaching out for one another; a need for understanding and for love.

For a long time they made love, but finally the heat, the passion, the animal emotions welling in them subsided, and they parted, their bodies tired but satisfied.

As he lay back quietly smoking a cigarette he realized that he loved her. He knew what she was; she'd told him that the night before. It didn't matter. Everybody was allowed a few mistakes in life. He'd made some of his own. So she'd had a bad time in the big town. A pretty girl in trouble; it was the same old story.

Hell, he'd not lived such a clean life. Jockeying contra-band; smuggling. And God knew what Big Dave had called him in to use his plane for; but that didn't matter now!

He looked at the girl. He'd known her only a few hours, but he loved her; you got to know something about people. He liked this woman. He didn't like Dave. But he realized what would happen if Dave found out about them.

An adult knew what he wanted in a woman. And after a while, he could tell in a glance.

It had been mutual love at first sight. That happened, sometimes. Though never to him before this. It was as if they were soul-mates who had known one another in past lives, and upon meeting in this one had instantly recognized that soul so deeply hidden. What each of them had done up to that moment of meeting meant little. They belonged to one another; and always would, throughout eternity.

Hell, he didn't know why that might be. But he was con-vinced..

He wanted this woman. He wanted her more than any-body else.

And here, in Big Dave's town, it would be sure death to ever see her again.

"I love you!" he said suddenly.

"I guess silly...but I feel the same way."

He could tell by the worried look in her blue eyes just how confused she was. He could see that she must feel the same emotions he felt; she must, or she wouldn't have come to him like this.

"Last night..." she said, sitting up and looking at him seriously, "Last night I felt something...and I was sure you must too...it's funny...but something seemed to click..."

"I didn't like it at first...it scared me."

"But I couldn't stay away. I had to see you, and I had to!"

"To find out the truth?" Barry offered, tenderly.

"Yes."

"I felt I'd go mad; you left without even letting me know your name..."

"Joan Withers," she smiled. "I thought it might just be a passing animal attraction...passion...now I don't..."

104

"*I know it wasn't!*"

"*I know; what are we going to do?*"

"*Don't really...can't...maybe we should leave town to-gether...*"

"*I couldn't. Dave would just send one of his boys after us...*"

"*Hell! Leave the country!*"

He was shocked by his own words. He was shocked by the decision which his mind had already made. He wanted her. He was going to have her!

Grabbing hold of her shoulders he exclaimed: "*I don't know why...I don't even know how it happened; or how last-ing it will be...or real my emotions for you are I don't think it really matters. I want you and you say you feel the same way! We're adults...I love you now...I want you more than anything else in the world...I'm willing to fight for you...to get you out of here. 0...Hell! You can't be worse off with me than with Dave.*"

She leaned over closer to him, sliding her arms around his neck, and moving her cheek to his. "*Oh, God...I've never felt such a need for anyone before, I want you the same way you want me...regardless of what comes out of it later.*"

She clutched to him. Her breath shortened. Her lips crushed on his, soft and moist, desperately seeking, anx-iously demanding.

The horrible desperation returned, flooding over them. He felt the muscles in her go rigid with excitement, as she moved up against him harder.

"*Oh, love me...love me...my dear wonderful love!*" she sighed, wildly working her mouth on his neck. Her teeth bit into the flesh of his shoulder as a moan of helpless excite-ment rippled through her body convulsively.

He ran his hands over her trembling form, and her skin went fiery under his touch.

Her fingers clawed his back, and her mouth sought his again. Her tongue reached out in a surge of hungry anxiety.

The wildness, the savage demands, the burning fervor bathed over their bodies, numbing all thoughts, all reason, all memory. Only the desire, that had to be fulfilled, only the love that was so needed, only the heated awareness of two *lovers who have discovered themselves, each other existed. And then final union.*

They did not stop.

They could not.

It as a moment of ecstasy that seemed to last forever, but finally came to an end.

He looked down at her lovely face and smiled tenderly. "I love you...oh, how I love you."

He kissed her lightly.

"There's no question about what we must do, now," he said sternly. "It's settled! We leave...get out of this damn city...and then out of the country...the plane's fueled...it's ready. All we have to do is leave!"

She smiled up at him. She said nothing. She didn't have to.

He knew.

She would come. She was his now.

There was a suddenly knocking on the door.

Barry jerked upright, then froze.

He saw Joan's eyes go wide with terror, and her body shudder.

Who could it be?

"Open up, Flyboy!" a hard, high pitched man's voice demanded.

That's when the first horror started. Tommy. Big Dave's gunman.

Now they faced another horror.

Barry turned the wheel of the car, and directed the vehicle through the gate that enclosed the air field.

Now it was a case of getting his plane into the air before Big Dave came storming along with his insane anger, his determination to kill.

It took what seemed forever for Barry to check out his plane, pay for the housing of it, and have it pulled out of the hanger.

Once the four-seat plane was free of the hanger, Barry warmed up the engines, explaining to Joan how to strap herself in.

He called the control tower, and was getting instructions

106

for the take off when Big Dave arrived.

Things happened fast then.

A car pulled out of the night, right in front of the plane, blocking its pathway.

Two men got out of the front seat. One was tall, the other short and heavy. Two others piled out of the back seat.

"Big Dave!" Joan cried as she saw the short fact man.

"Latch the doors quickly!" Barry yelled hand her the gun he had taken from Big Dave's man. "Use it if necessary."

He checked over the controls. Then he threw aside the mike, knowing the control taking off without instructions; there just wasn't time to do anything but move fast.

He had to think of some way to get around the car; or they would never make it.

"Get down..." he demanded, as the four men came running toward the plane.

He throttled the engine, then moved the control stick.

He'd have to take a chance!

Slowly the plane moved.

A shot rang out, and the glass splattered between the two of them.

Joan leaned out the door, at her side, and returned the man's fire.

Her aim was terrible.

The plane moved closer to the car.

Touched it.

The wing was clearing, but the cockpit, and body scraped the car.

Barry felt a sickening fear run through him.

They weren't going to make it!

One of the men was reaching up to the cockpit door, near Joan. A gun was pointing through the glass.

He had to move fast!

Joan screamed and fired at the face. It jumped backwards, yelling in pain.

He'd have to chance it.

He pressed the throttle.

Another bullet crashed through the cockpit, grazing the back of his head. He felt nausea flood over him. Blackness started to cover his vision. He shook his head and fought for awareness.

A scraping sounded, and then it turned into a loud grating noise.

We aren't making it. We aren't going to make it, his mind screamed.

His vision was clearing, and his mind was beginning to work more efficiently.

The grating sound ended, and the plane moved forward.

Another bullet exploded past them, just missing Joan.

The sound of more bullets hitting glass and metal surrounded them. But they were clear of the car.

He pointed the plane toward the dark runway, and kept going; he didn't have time to consult the control tower. He could only hope for the best.

And as they left the shrill sound of the bullets and soared into the sky, the passengers Barry and Joan let out a sigh of relief seconds before the two planes collided.

His last thought was: maybe their souls would meet again, soon, and rediscover one another under better circumstances. Maybe next time it would last for a life time.

Death came quick and painlessly, and Big Dave was cheated.

෨FITTE THE EIGHTEENTHଙ

This is one of the liquor articles which I had published during this time. It is my special History of Rum. This is a about the charms of rum and how it can be used to create a seductive mood for a romantic night for a couple in love. Or, at the very least, a night of mutual pleasure, if you happened to be a would-be pirate with a lovely maiden on hand to go off on a South Sea Island adventure. That's when you...

SAY RUM, CHUMଙ

Anytime anybody thinks of a fancy, out-of-this-world drink they will invariably come up with a mental picture of some rum drink. There are several reasons for this; and most of them are pretty good and understandable. Rum drinks have the hint of tropics and therefore the hint of romance and passion which will delight any lovely female and help to bring her into a more willingly seductive mood.

Once, when having a friend over for a dinner and entertainment, and a few drinks, the subject came up as to what had been put into the "cocktail that I'd mixed her with." It would seem, from her reactions, that something had hit her right between the eyes like an exploding atomic bomb, sending colorful stars in all directions and she couldn't see how it had all been done. She said it made her feel so warm and gay—and she wasn't talking about the weather or anything short of an inner feeling to be affectionate and show her pleasure at having been put in the "right mood." The simple answer was, naturally, rum.

There is nothing like rum in the world, when it comes to making a strong drink with hidden power-drivers, or making a good tasting drink which all will enjoy, regardless of their tastes in liquor.

Today, rum is thought of in combinations such as the *zombie,* which a rather sharp restaurant owner created for the pleasure of his customers. Today, Don the Beachcomber is almost as famous as the drink he originated.

But rum has had a long and interesting history which is connected with literature, pirates and rum-runners, that gives it more than a mere romantic flavor to the taste buds.

> *"Fifteen men on a Dead Man's Chest—*
> *Yo-ho-ho and a bottle of rum!*
> *Drink and the devil had done for the rest—*
> *Yo-ho-ho and a bottle of rum!"*

Robert Louis Stevenson wasn't just writing a few lyrical lines of fantasy for his book *Treasure Island,* when he created those now famous verses for his bearded and deadly pirates to sing while downing bottle upon bottle of this dark brown liquor which was their favorite "man's" drink. He was taking a truth of life about these rugged men of the high seas and recording down for history and literature the devotion which these daring men had for this distilled sugar byproduct.

There must be some reason why these pirates of the high seas, swinging their cutlasses and cursing at their hard lives and hard living and fighting and loving, went so strongly for this dark-brown, heavy boiled liquor called rum. There must be some reason why rum's history saw men like Sir Henry Morgan, Spanish explorers of the New World, smugglers, pirates, and during the recent Prohibition era, "rum-runners." One finds it had to picture a bottle of rum without getting the feeling of the romantic hard living and hard men and hard loving which helped to open the New World: or tropical islands with Spanish- and French- and English-speaking sailors.

Yet today the drink of the pirates fits just as boldly and naturally in the hearts of modern drinking habits, as it did for the hearty seamen, with such ever popular drinks as the *zombie* and the Daiquiri Cocktail, or just the old pirate stand-by—a straight bottle of rum.

There is nothing more delightful, pleasant to the taste, or versatile to the bartender, than rum; there isn't a thing that can't be downed with this liquor of the pirates, when it comes to mixing new and delightful taste treats. It can be used in cooking, as well as drinking; it can be taken straight, it can be mixed with wines, other liquors and liqueurs, fruit juices of all kinds or used as a flavoring for candies, cakes or food.

Rum is a product which is distilled from the fermented juices of sugar cane or any other by-product of sugar or molasses. It is an alcoholic beverage whose origin has been somewhat faded to time, but still believed to have deriver from a far Asian country; still, wherever it did originate, there is no doubt about where it is loved and drunk and produced today, or the romantic history which it became a part of during the opening of the New World, and later at the time in American history when it was illegal to produce and sell and type or kind of liquor for public use.

There are several stories related to the origin of the name rum, any of which could have some truth to them. One tells of the swashbuckling adventurers who called it "rumbustion" and "Rumbullion"; and another claims it was named for Admiral Vernon, who saved his men from dying of scurvy by giving them this new East Indian beverage in place of their daily beer ration.

Still, there is even a more logical seeming answer to how it was named, in the story which is believed by many people still living in the tropics: it is said that thousands of years ago the Hindus had a work for sugar, *sakkara,* which was later changed for Latin use into *saccharum.* When man and science and drinkers got their heads together to create something new and exciting for the drinking public they came up with the word "rum" by just dropping the first six letters of this Latin word for sugar. All in all it would seem possible that each story might be, in some degree, part of the truth. But today it doesn't really matter much which is or isn't the full truth, for regardless of what you call it, there is nothing like this drink of the pirates in the world.

Rum is basically cheap to produce and in countries like Mexico, can be bought for as little as $1.25 a fifth. But a good bottle can be obtained here in the States for something close to four dollars on up to nine dollars a fifth (depending on brand, type, color, aroma, strength, texture, and age). There are hundreds of brands and about a dozen types of rum, but this never confuses the expert, for he learns to enjoy each and every type, by themselves or combined together and with other liquors and liqueurs and fruit juices. One thing most people don't realize is that blending several types of rum and kinds and brands of rum makes the drink much better. Instead of just using one kind of rum, the secret is to use several types, giving the drink a fuller, richer, and more well-rounded flavor.

Each brand naturally has its own standards and levels of quality, but even then there are only the following popular types—and sometimes these will be different in degree of quality. Barbados, Cuban, Demerara, Jamaican, Martinique, New England, Puerto Rican, Virgin Islands, Haitian, Habañero, Philippine, Batavia Arak, Trinidad, and Venezuelan. Unlike other spirits, Rum can be bought with as high a proof as 151 (200 proof would be 100% alcohol), which is used as a topping for Zombies and other rum drinks of this type. Rum comes dark or light; the darker many times being heavier in body, yet this is not always the rule, since the difference can also be only in the coloring which has been added to darken it.

Good grade rum is a delight to taste when taken straight in a liqueur or shot glass. Sipped slowly, it reveals its inner perfection and own individual taste. But, also several rums can be combined to make a blend of each of their flavors, giving an all-over effect which is even more delightful and rewarding.

In the mixing of Rum punches and zombies one quickly discovers the need of having several brands and types and proofs of run. Generally such drinks will be Puerto Rican, Jamaican, Demerara and Cuban; the most common rums used and sometimes Virgin Islands rum will be called for. This does not mean a person shouldn't use some of the others, if they are on hand. In fact, it is a good idea, when making a rum drink, to first mix a "rum-base." What you do is to combine the rums together beforehand, and then after finding out the amount of liquor the drink calls for, measuring an equal proportion of the "rum-base"—it not only makes the drink easier to mix, but also gives it your own personal touch.

There are several advantages in mixing a rum drink, rather than buying the many rum fruit mixes being marketed today. One it that you can make a strong, but good-tasting cocktail or punch or cooler or Collins or zombie, and it will be hard to tell it from fruit juice or soft drinks. Or you can make one hell of a knock-out bomb, and all you think you are drinking is something delightfully strong, rummy-tasting—until it hits you (or the girl) like an atomic bomb! Also, rum will mix with almost any other liquor or liqueur or fruit juice so beautifully that one would think they had originally been created to be blended together.

In the mixing of any good rum drink, as with any other drink, it is necessary to follow only a few easy to remember rules:

1. Always pour the liquors over the ice. This will chill the liquor without watering it down any more than necessary.
2. Chill your glasses first—before mixing drinks.
3. Serve icy drinks as quickly as possible to avoid dilution.
4. Use fresh fruit, if possible.
5. Get the best liquor you can afford.
6. Stir drinks only, never shake—unless told to do so.

There are other fine points in the mixing of drinks and the know ledge comes in time, for it is in the Personal touch of your own taste and creative ability.

Any bar book will tell you how to mix a good Daiquiri or a Ruin Collins, Rum Sour, Planter's Punch, Rum Ricky, Rum Gimlet, Hot Toddy Rum, Hot Buttered Rum, Tom and Jerry, or Rum and 7-Up. What they won't tell you is how to mix some of the following rum delights which have been found, by the author, to be some of the most exciting experiences into the delights of drinking pleasure, and the sensual pleasure which the women are anxious to give in reward for the good drink they have been served with. All of them should be made with the highest quality liquor and the freshest of fruit and fruit juice—don't use canned juice if you are able to get fresh juice.

Two simple drinks are Coconut & Rum and Ginger Rum. The Coconut & Rum is but a combination of one jigger of any rum which you might like with the addition of coconut milk; they should be poured over ice, garnished with a cherry and sipped through a straw. The second drink, Ginger Rum, is made up of one ounce of Ginger Brandy and one jigger of light Cuban rum. Pour over ice cubes in high-ball glass, add two teaspoons of grenadine and then fill with soda. Sip through straws and garnish with cherry. Both drinks are simple to make and delightful to drink.

If you want something for the hot afternoon which is little stronger, try a Caribbean Cooler. This is not only relaxing but also a drink which everybody will want to have more of. And naturally this calls for seconds which will please any bartender, for he knows that he'd done what he set out to do in the first place—and the woman ill be soon quite willing to show her delight, by delighting him with the curving giving softness of her body and kisses. The drink is simple enough to make, but gives the impression that you have gone to a lot of bother to produce a not only good tasting drink, but also a good looking one, too. First, take a Collins glass and fill it half full of crushed ice and then add the following: 1 ounce Puerto Rican rum, one ounce vodka, one ounce Sloe Gin, the juice of one-half lime. Stir with sizzle sick until mixture is completely chilled and then fill with soda water, stir again and then add cherry, slice of lime and mint sprig. Place a couple of straws into this Caribbean Cooler, and serve. The flavor will be delicate but strong enough to disguise the liquor taste. It is a perfect choice for the person who doesn't like the taste of liquor too much, but enjoys the effects.

But for the drinker who likes the flavor of liquor more or less straight, yon might try something like Jamaican Sunset. This is a pleasant blend of the national drink of Mexico, Tequila, and the produce of the isle of Jamaica, flavored with a

114

touch of lemon juice and a dash of liqueur.

After filling an old fashioned glass with ice cubes, add the following:

One ounce Tequila, one jigger Jamaica Rum, the juice of one-half lemon, and one ounce of Maraschino liqueur. Stir gently, fill with soda water, and then garnish with a maraschino cherry. This will delight anybody who has a yearning to feel the hot passion of Mexico and Jamaica flow through their veins. It's a fiery drink which is good on a warm evening, for it is cooling and relaxing and inwardly warming.

But there is really only *one* summer drink which is always thought of when one sees a bottle of rum:

The Zombie! It is a mystery drink which the owner of Don the Beach-corner restaurant seems determined to keep as a secret.

Place into a shaker several ice cubes and then add the following: one ounce White Puerto Rican rum, one ounce Jamaica rum, one ounce Dark Virgin Island rum, one ounce Demerara rum, one-half ounce apricot (or peach) liqueur, one ounce of Crème de Almond, juice of one-half lime and one ounce pineapple juice. Now shake the devil out of it until well blended and chilled. Then pour into fourteen-ounce zombie glass, quarter-filled with crushed ice. Garnish with slice of lime, a sprig of mint and one maraschino cherry. Top with a small layer (about one-eighth to a quarter inch) of 151 proof Demerara rum and then serve with straws. This will send any lovely lady into the happy hunting grounds of passion, back across time into the Caribbean and the swashbuckling days when rum was the drink of pirates.

After two of these zombies and any man will feel like lifting his beautiful woman into his arms and carrying her off onto the high seas (or someplace else where they will find the privacy which is so important for the survival of what wonderful feeling that can only be expressed in the arms of two people in love).

You won't have to say, "yo-ho-ho and a bottle of rum!" Since for all practical effects, you've already had your seaman's quote, and are adventuring on the Spanish Main with a girl in your arms, a drink in hand, and love in your heart.

And all this for the price of a few bottles of rum, and the

art of knowing how to mix and handle the drink of the hearty pirates. Good pirating; good drinking, and good loving.

✂FITTE THE NINETEENTH✃

And another one of those special fluffy wonders, ladies of great virtue who resist seductive traps, until, or unless, the man discovers the secret key to her loving embraces and loving kisses, and lovely, wonderful body. Like all idealistic ladies of deep convictions, Clara was a major challenge. In order to possess her she demanded something very special:

THE 21ˢᵗ STEP✃

"Well, the way I see it she's just not that kind of girl!" Bill Carter announced. "But I plan on making the most of her twenty-first birthday tonight!"

"Seduction?" Ralph Daily argued, lifting from his chair several inches.

"If at all possible!" he announced.

"Considering your track record, maybe. But she's a very resistant young lady. I mean everybody has tired to score with her, and been blown away, no hits no run and all errors!"

"I think she's like any other woman. Clara is just as easy as any other girl...you just have to push the right button..."

This time Ralph stood completely. He moved across the room toward the window and looked out into the yard which extended two hundred feet outwards, until it ended in a gigantic stone wall. "Your trouble is you think you can seduce any lady."

"Only those who willingly want to be seduced. You just go through a certain routine...like taking twenty-one steps...at

117

the twenty-first, she'll give in..."

Ralph turned and looked around at the other man. "Just don't take that last step though...that's the marriage step...and knowing you, that's a no-no! I call it the twenty-first step because it is much like the same gigantic step one takes when they turn twenty-one: total freedom! But in reverse. For a man, instead of gaining his freedom he loses it! I'm not quite sure what the twenty-first is for a woman!"

"Okay, Mister Ralph Daily!" Bill said, stepping toward his friend. "I'll make you a bet...that I don't have to take that twenty-first step to get Clara Worthington in bed! And tonight I'll find the way to convince her how wonderful it can be!"

Ralph brightened happily. "I'll take that bet!"

* * * * * * *

Clara Worthington was one of those girls who believe that the bed is only for marriage, and that kissing should confine itself to a gentle good-night touching of the lips. *Nothing more!*

Even if this was her twenty-first birthday! This was her birthday gift. For weeks she had wanted to go out with Bill Carter. It didn't change anything. But being out with this lovely man was such a wonderful experience. He'd been everything a woman might wish for in so many ways. Exciting, yet a gentleman in a powerful way.

Bill Carter was so deliciously all man, almost aggressive. But so charming, so delightful, so thrilling. Just being with him all evening long had been a wonderful tease. And when they dance, after dinner and cocktails, she was totally swept off her feet. He held her so close. And she could tell how stimulating he found her. That was almost embarrassing, even if in a way flattering. Bill Carter had quite a reputation with the ladies. But for some reason he seemed so honest, so down the earth, very real.

When he said "You are the most lovely woman I have ever been with," she found it impossible not to believe him. Maybe she simply wanted to believe.

But his shoulders were so broad and while dancing she

118

couldn't help feeling the really very hard muscles of his arms, where her fingers clung tight. A bit later in the evening he brought her body so very close, put both his arms around her waist and she willingly, deliciously, clung to him, her own arms sliding about his neck. It was so thrilling to feel his manly form so close and so totally exciting in just about every imaginable way.

Her mind was dizzy with the cocktails and the dancing and the lovely conversation which had covered just about every possible subject, including a now and then compliment about her lovely hair, her bright eyes, the curve of her full red lips. His compliments were delicious. She was almost drunk from those lovely words.

Of course, realistically, she realized that men found her very attractive. She never fooled herself about that. But to hear it said to her in such a passionate manner, with such convincing words, voice, and oh, those looks as his eyes met hers. She almost swooned for the total effect. She was terrified about what might happen if he really turned on the pressure with all that charm and magnificent sexual power behind it.

She steeled herself to resist with all her power. Regardless of anything he might say or do, she would not give in. She was determined about that.

She knew her effect on men. It had been obvious since she turned fifteen. And as she matured she became very popular.

She was a beautiful blonde, who knew more about dressing than anyone else. She could wear a tight fitting sweater and full skirt and look better than any other girl.

She had firmer breast material than all girls wrapped up into one. Her waist was so narrow that viewed sideways, it didn't seem to exist at all. Her hips were round curving lines that tempted any man's fingers to want to follow.

But no man ever touched.

Well, not, really. Maybe while dancing, like Bill had been doing to her all evening. But that was different; a kind of delicious tease.

Look...but don't touch! her eyes had always had a habit to flash meaningfully. And that's all any male did. One

119

glance at her long, sharp fingernails assured any man that it would be slightly dangerous to ever get near.

It's not to be assumed that she was a dead head. Not in the least. Clara was more popular than other young woman. For that matter there were hardly any other females, anywhere, that were more popular.

To see her was to fall in love.

And it was obvious that Bill wanted to do more than hold hands at mid-night under an August moon. He, naturally, had seductive designed on her body; that was apparent from the first moments of their date. And it had continued to be more painfully alive and powerful as the evening had progressed.

In the car next to him, she found it difficult to avoid looking at the man; wondering what it might be actually like to be married to him. Under those circumstanced, of course, they would be lovers.

Yet she felt like he was her lover this evening. In a way he had made verbal love time and again, and his body had surged so thrillingly against hers that it was like being bathed of ecstasy.

Could she resist him?

He brought the car to stop. It was only than that she realized he'd taken her up to the hills overlooking the town. It was known by some as "lover's lane".

Oh, God, he really did have designs on her body.

He turned, and before she even realized what was happening, his eyes were feasting on her, caressing across her body, and then sudden he swept her into his arms.

It was then that she stiffened. Frantically. She couldn't let him seduce her; this was supposed to be only a teasing job on her part, not a sexual orgy! Well, nothing beyond maybe a good night kiss or something like that.

She stiffened into a rigid stone hardness.

"Stop! *Please!*" she hissed, much too loud!

"What's wrong?" he murmured. "I think you are so wonderful. I simply want to envelop you into my arms."

"You shouldn't do that," she warned.

"Why?"

"Well, really, Bill. Isn't it quite obvious?"

120

"No. To be truthful we both desire one another. I've never been with any woman whom I've desired more than you." His voice was choked with passion.

"I'm a nice lady and a woman who values her virtue!" she stated, feeling instantly foolish.

"Oh, come on baby...you know you want it!" he said, squeezing her thigh cruelly.

A stab of excitement ran through her. Maybe just playing along for a bit might not be too bad. It wasn't as if she would go all the way, of course. She did want more than holding hands and conversation.

Turning, she looked up at him. "I'm not that kind of girl! You know that!" Her voice was quivering. She tried to control it, but it didn't do any good. She was shaky clean through.

"Oh, come on...don't give me that virgin stuff!" he demanded, moving his hand higher on her leg, close to the sacred center of her treasures.

"Don't!" she snapped, reaching down and moving his hand forcefully away. His fingers clasped hers and they felt warm and soft. She liked the feel of them. She liked him a lot

"And I am a virgin!" she cried, feeling confused, and then silly because she had said it. "Well, damn it all, what's wrong with being a virgin?"

He laughed and shrugged. "You said it, baby...not me!"

"I mean it! What's wrong!" she didn't know why she was forcing the subject. She didn't want to talk about it. But she couldn't help herself.

Was she looking for some excuse, some rationalization? Hardly, her mind argued.

Hot flashes were running through her. Making her dizzy. She burned terribly.

"Nothing wrong really...if that's what you really want to be." His words and tone of voice were icy and jagged.

"Well I am! Damn it!"

She was suddenly mad. And she didn't know why. Why should she, be mad?

After all, all her life she had been a nice girl. She hadn't allowed men to caress her, or kiss her the way other girls let them do.

121

But. She didn't have any right to be excited. It wasn't nice. It wasn't right. Well, not as excited at Bill Carter made her feel. She wanted to run her finger tips along his manly muscles and to hold him close, to feel the two of them skin to skin.

Oh, what a shocking idea that was! Where did it come from? She wondered about that. Such evil thoughts.

A girl should keep sex for marriage.

Why?

Because that was what she had been told all her life. Of course, it was right. Completely right. Morals. One had to live by morals! But was it really immoral? After all she was an adult; not a child any more.

She felt him squeezing her body closer to him in a friendly, but seductive way. It felt nice, and she found herself pushing in against him.

It was so obvious, and impossible to hide her true feelings form this wonderfully exciting man when he looked deeply into her eyes.

"See you want it, too!" he smiled, turning her toward him, and looking down into her eyes. "But you're afraid! Aren't you?"

She couldn't speak. She was afraid too speak. Afraid of what she would *say.*

"You shouldn't be, for it is just as natural as breathing. It was as if we were made for one another. This night, the moon is bright, the evening has been perfection. And now, here we are, together, and we both long for one another. I feel that so strongly."

Suddenly she wanted to be kissed. Kissed real hard, and long and very deep!

That thought shocked her. It was all wrong.

"You're twenty-one," he smiled knowingly, "you're an adult. What a woman...for God's sake what are you really saving it for? There's nothing wrong with sex if you know how to take care of yourself afterwards."

She did; but then any girl that could read knew about such things.

"No...no, please!" she pleaded.

Her face was flushed. Her lips trembling. Her eyes suddenly closed.

She looks like an angel, he thought, reaching down and kissing her lips softly. They pressed up eagerly. Then they withdrew fearfully.

He forced them back, and this time he kissed her hard and violently. With one hand he gently urged her mouth open. It hesitated, then finally the lips parted, as if suddenly she had made up her mind; or it had been made up for her.

After that it was easy, terribly easy.

Later, locked in each others arms, she sighed contentedly, and pressed closer to her lover. It had been nice, she thrilled inwardly. So very nice.

After all, she was over twenty-one and had finally taken that last step to maturity, and was glad.

The twenty-first step!

꧁FITTE THE TWENTIETH꧂

Sometimes it's music to your ears, sometimes to your feet, and for some people it becomes a wild concerto of movement so sensual that it leaves a fella breathless. Well that kinda suggests what our hero was up against when he met the…

ROCK 'N' ROLL SWEETHEART꧂

Jerry Parsons was feeling a little depressed. He had good reason; he hadn't had a girl for several weeks. Not that he was a sex fiend. Just that he liked women and not to be making with the jollies with one or the other was rather upsetting.

He was normal.

Well, tonight, he thought, he would do something about it!

Normally he would have called up some girl he knew, but most of his favorite women were either out of town, out, period—as far as he was concerned—or tied up with other men.

So he had to resort to the thing he hated worst of all; a pick-up joint. The place he chose was a rock 'n' roll spot not far from his apartment. That would make things easy, just in case he was able to pick up something; only a hop, skip and a jump from his private mating room.

Things were really swinging at the place. That is if you like Rock 'n' Roll. But more than that, the girls were really bump and twistin' like crazy. Put another way, real swingerios!

And Jerry Parsons liked swingerios!

When that rock 'n' roll beat started filling the room, the girls with the wildest hips started with the action and it wasn't long before he himself was starting with the jazzy moves. Like he started asking a couple of girls—one at a time—to make with the swinging!

Man, they real ripped up the rug. Wailed like crazy!

That's all good and fine, but he hadn't come to dance; at least not in that way! He had come to find himself a hot woman that really blew a wild chorus, of a completely different type, and hungry to go to his mating room, back at the apartment.

Like he wanted to make one hop and skip and leap into her naked arms.

So he was keeping his eyes out for that certain smile to come his way.

The funny thing he found it every once in a while; on the wrong person.

Like that fat, ugly woman in the corner, with her large eager eyes.

Or that one over there, with the flat chest.

There was a likely maiden, who looked his way. She had beautiful hair, a pretty smile

Cod-fish!

What horrible lips.

Then another young chick caught his eyes. She was cute.

The music blared from the bandstand.

Her eyes asked the question.

Let's dance!

Let's wail! he answered, taking hold of her arm and angling over to the floor where several couples were already making with the swinging.

Never had he seen such a thing. He was flattened out into the hottest pan-cake in the world.

Just watching her swingeroo hippies making the whing whammies made his head dizzy. What bounceronies of flesh kittens!

After the dance was completed and he was able to start recovering with a drink, he looked deep into her eyes with the old sure stuff.

Like, I know you like me, and I like you, so let's not play games, was his silent signal, his implied invitation. *We're adults, and you know what I want, and I know what you want, so let's get with it?*

So he came right out with it!

"Let's cut and then blast up to my place for a couple of wild thrills."

She nodded sexily, bobbed her "kittens," smiled, and said: "Keep it awhile. Just got here, and like to dance."

Crazy!

Made in the shade?

So they danced.

And the way her body wailed to the music would put Slick Vanny and his muscle building organization out of business. He was exercising his eyes, just following her body acting. What eye exercise!

Like, he'd have the most developed eyes in the world if they did many dances like this.

Suddenly the music stopped, the lights dimmed and the combo played slow romantic sex-stuff.

Man, what a pair of "kittens" to have smashed into his chest.

He did.

What a body to crush into his.

He did.

Sliding both arms around her waist he gave her a little squeeze which really flattened her against him.

She moaned excitedly and slid her arms around his neck. He felt her lips slip around his ear and the moistness of her tongue work with the lobe.

Like dizzy!

Then the hippies. Slip and slide, little whams and bams.

They started with the jazz stuff, right against his, hard, fast, forceful, anxious excitement.

He could hardly stand it. Or, rather, stand, period.

Like, hop, skip and jump—that was what he wanted. But she wasn't with that like of music, yet.

She seemed to like working her hips against his, and biting his ear-lobe and wiggling her "kittens" on his chest, and caressing his neck with her fingers.

126

Crazy, dad.

But too crazy.

Like, how much can a guy take?

Or, rather, how much can a guy stand?

He was finding out.

Finally the hell stopped.

The dance ended.

"Like, let's flip out?" he suggested.

She smiled and pushed her hips hard against his, and then worked them in a sorta crazy kind of way that made his brain sizzle and smash outwards against his skull like an insane ape trying to escape its cage.

"Let's stay awhile," she hoarsely said in such a low-down filled-with-sex kind of voice that he couldn't speak for a moment to argue with her, and by that time they were rock 'n' rolling again.

Swingerios!

Hippie whippiest.

Kittens—flatten!

Whing, whang!

Bang!

The kittens sorta tried to knock each other out as they forcefully smashed against one another.

Whing, whang!

Double-bang!

The eyes in his sockets were whinging and whanging in time with her "kittens" and he couldn't stop them.

She smiled, parted her lips, moistened them with her tongue, then gave with the sex in her large eyes and banged her body against his. Then she moved back a little, then …

Bang, again!

It was getting to be too much.

"Like let's flip!"

She moved against him again, and gave out with the excitement. "Like sure!"

Like dad crazy!

So there, they were.

In his apartment.

But she had changed. Completely different.

Quiet. Calm. Cool.

Cold, in fact!

"Like baby, what's with you?" he demanded after having kissed her hard, tightly sealed lips and playing with her "kittens."

She looked up at him with a strange look in her eyes. "What you mean?" she asked in surprise.

"Well, get with it. Like flip. Start whaling. Swingerino it a little!"

"Like what?" she demanded sitting up in the bed and looking hard and cold at him.

What a delightful body she had. Large kittens. Mountains that were the highest he had ever explored or climbed.

Narrow waist. Round, flaring, silky smooth hips; long full thighs.

But she didn't use them.

"Like swing. You know, squirm. Respond! Wiggle! Shake! Make with the sex!"

Her expression was puzzled; then she brightened up a bit. "Oh, you mean swing?" She swung for a moment. "Like that?"

"Like that!"

"Gotta have music for that kind of stuff!"

"Music?"

"Music!" she demanded.

He squeezed one of her kittens.

She didn't so much as act as if he had done anything to her. He kissed her long and hard, but her lips remained sealed.

"Swing, damn you!" he cursed, really making with the sex—stuff, caressing those portions of her that were sure to make her eagerly swing.

It didn't.

"I'm a rock 'n' roll sweetheart!" she laughed after he tried several other means of getting her excited.

That did it.

Rock 'n' roll it would be.

He got up, went to the record player and put a record album on.

The moment the music started, she started. Man, like this is going to be a swinging session, he thought, slipping down beside her jerking and "swinging" body.

It was.

Which all goes to prove that when it comes to a rock 'n' roll sweetheart, you do it with music!

Some girls just have to hear the sound of music to understand what this thing called love really is.

When it comes to a rock 'n' roll sweetheart, you gotta whistle a little tune; if you don't have it there, you don't get it!...where it counts the most!

℘FITTE THE TWENTY-FIRST℘

There's always a price tag. And sometimes it is pretty high, and sometimes it is pretty low, and sometimes it can be just right on. This little bit of fluff involves a delightful lady...

THE SIZZLE GIRL℘

She worked at the *Hot Spot,* a strip joint in the middle of Los Angeles. She was featured as the *Sizzle Girl.*

That was all that Larry Forrest knew about her, outside of the show she put on, and the beautiful shape of her body.

He was out with the boys at the office on a spree one night; the first time he saw her. It was one of those affairs where everybody got drunk and the married men tried to act like they were single and the single ones tried to act like men about town.

An awkward affair where everything was dizzy and lightly out of focus.

Everything, that is, except the *Sizzle Girl.*

The minute she came on the stage the whole audience went wild. She had a long, voluptuous body that didn't know where to stop. Her breasts started at her chest and then bulged outwards, and outwards, and then further outwards. They didn't bag or sag. Just straight and rigid balls of flesh that became tremendous beacons and excitement.

Her waist was almost not there. It pinched in so narrow that it was easy to miss.

Then her hips started.

No...blasted out! One great circle that slid down into the

130

fullest, roundest thighs that Larry had ever seen.

He knew his eyes were bugging. But he didn't care.

His hands were nervously working like running spider legs, wiggling and intertwining madly. A hot chill quivered through him as he watched one piece of clothing come off after another.

The slow first chorus that did away with the gloves and the hat and finally the outer dress.

Then the faster dance that bumped and ground until his insides were burning with an ache that was terrible.

The bathing suit type of affair came off and she stood almost naked before them. Only stars barely hiding the tips of her nipples. Only a miniature G-string to keep the show legal.

Then the dancing really became fierce. Her hips swung and banged as if they were on hinges. Her breasts circled and bounced, banged together, flew apart...swing, swang, whang, bang!

There wasn't a thing she couldn't do with those fantastically large flesh-balls. One at a time or both together.

Every inch of her dancing like wild. Then suddenly it was over.

He felt weak. Helpless. Out of breath. Exhausted.

Never had he seen such a thing. Never had he experienced such a thing. Never had there been such a thing as ...

The Sizzle Girl!

That night in bed he couldn't get the image of her bouncing figure out of his mind.

Those delightful breasts...*if only to play catch with a pair like that!*

It made his mind drop into a deep red well that seemed to have no end.

Then suddenly he hit bottom and there she was, swinging her hips, swaying her body.

She had nothing on.

She came at him, rolling her hips seductively. Her eyes flaming with hot promise. Her breasts banging together, swinging back and forth; her whole body writhing. Her lips parted and opened wider and wider and wider, until a great canyon was existing before him. It was gigantic. Big enough to put his fist in; his arm; his head; and then finally his whole body. Then it was a huge valley. A monster tongue beckoned him in. And a deep voice exploded into being. "Come on in, my darling...my lover...my delightful..."

He started to move forward...

And then he awakened.

He was sweating. He was shaking. He was burning. His body was tangled in the covers and sheets.

He tried to smoke, but it didn't calm his nerves. Never had he had such a terrible dream.

He couldn't sleep the rest of the night.

It was impossible. And he couldn't get the girl out of his mind.

The next day she was in his every thought, until he couldn't even work. He went home early on the excuse of a headache.

That night without even knowing how he had gotten there, he discovered he had gone to the Hot Spot. He was fascinated with every show. She went through the same routine every time, but each time he saw some new delight; a new thrill; and a new excitement.

That night the same dream plagued him.

And he awakened at four and couldn't get back to sleep.

It was hell.

When he discovered himself at the club the next night and dreamed again the same dream, he became terrified.

He was worried about his job. His sanity.

His health.

In desperation he went to a friend of his who was a professional headshrinker.

"What's wrong with me, Harry?" he cried desperately. He was sweating terribly. Shaking. His head throbbed with horrible pains.

Harry-the-Headshrinker sat thoughtfully for a long time. He fingered his beard for a few moments, then looked sharply at Larry.

"Well, it's fairly simple."

"What...what is it? For heaven's sake, tell me...tell me...tell me!" he cried anxiously. He stood in his excitement and paced the floor of the small office.

132

"Get a date with the girl. It is fairly simple to see that you have a strong desire for this woman...and the only way to solve the problem is to get her...take her to bed if possible and explore the curves and delights of her body...and then you should never be bothered again..."

So, that was just what he planned. The very night. When the show was over he paid one of the waiters to send a message back stage that there was a man who wished to meet *The Sizzle Girl*.

The man returned regretful. "I'm sorry, but she can't make it."

His guts flipped inside him, making his stomach sick, he had to see her

Cold sweat poured out over him, oiling his body.

He had to see her!

He got up and walked toward the door at the side of the stage that was marked Private. He opened it. There was nobody around to stop him. He walked carefully along the small passageway that led to the back stage.

He looked around. Then saw what he was after. A dressing room door marked with a star, with the name *Miss Sizzle* on it.

He moved over to it. Knocked on it.

"Who's there?" a light, high voice called from behind the paneling.

He knocked again.

"Who's there?...oh, come on in, the door's open."

He opened it, stepped in and closed it after him.

Miss Sizzle was sitting at the dressing table combing her hair. When she saw his reflection she took in a deep breath of shock.

"Who're you?" she demanded, turning around and looking at him.

"I...I...I'm Larry Forrest!" he announced in a shaky low voice. He was burning all over.

Here she was, the girl of his nightmares. The body that had plagued him from the moment he had laid eyes on her.

He was breathing hard. Much too hard.

Terror filled her eyes.

He forced control over his nerves. His breathing returned to normal.

After all, he wasn't a savage. He was a normal man, who just happened to be fascinated by a fantastically sexy body. A body that he had to possess.

"Well, what the hell are you doing here?" Her face was hard and cold. Her eyes flashing ice. Her exciting body rigid. She stood.

"I...I just wanted to talk to you..." he finally managed to say.

"Are you a nut or something?" she asked, light concern shading her features. "Or sick? You all right?"

"Yeah...sure...I'm all right!" he assured her. "I just had to meet you and get acquainted. Please, let me talk...I'd love to take you out for something to eat, maybe?"

She paused as if suddenly struck by something. Her face became puzzled. She studied him for a long time and then finally shrugged. "If you don't mind paying the bill...I'll warn you that it'll cost..."

He couldn't believe his ears. It was too good to be true. Impossible?

And he couldn't care less about the price. Just to be with her and look at her and maybe touch her...and later, some-how, maybe make love to her!

The idea made him dizzy.

Twenty minutes later they were snacking at an expen-sive all-night restaurant.

She seemed as light and gay. Her body was revealed in its full splendor. It was almost like being on a date a girl he had known for months; an old friend.

When they had walked from her dressing room, she had taken hold of his arm and her touch had been all that he could have expected. And he was on fire from then on.

Since then they had touched hips and thighs and squeezed hands.

She seemed quite warm and affectionate.

"You know you're quite cute!" she giggled, reaching across the table and patting him on the hand. "I like you!" she exclaimed.

He had just told her how she had been affecting him in the past few days and she had squirmed and laughed

134

throughout the whole story like a delighted child—a delightful, grown-up sex-bomb! He hadn't been quite sure if she
were laughing at him or not until she had patted his hand.

"Would you like to come up to my apartment tonight?"
she asked suddenly.

He *couldn't believe his ears.*

"Yes! Oh, yes! If you don't mind...I mean..." he gulped
eagerly. "You know..."

Would he like to come to her apartment! He'd give almost anything.

She laughed. "Why should I mind? I like you. You are
fresh, and honest! After all, a working girl like me gets to
know men and people. You're okay!"

As they drove to her place he was almost in a dizzy
drunk. From the moment she had suggested they go there he
had been in a delightful intoxication. It was wonderful.

Her place was a small two-room affair, but plenty big
enough for the action they planned.

"Would you like a drink?" she offered, indicating a
small portable bar in the corner. "Help yourself and mix me
something...any old thing, as long as it's strong!"

He walked to the corner and fixed the drinks. He could
hear her moving around her room behind him. The sound of
switches being clicked was suggestive. And then the lighting
of the room changed to a dim glow. After that a bongo type
music started filling the air.

He turned. Then jolted in surprise.

She didn't have a stitch of clothing on.

And what glory!

She was swaying gently to the music.

"You like me?" she asked, taking the drink.

"Like crazy!" he managed to gulp out. He took several
swallows of the drink.

She downed hers in one big movement.

Then her body started to sway a little more to the music.

"Like sit down and enjoy the show!" she cried in a low
voice, indicating the sofa in front of her.

He sat, fascinated by the flowing movement of her body.

Her hips.

Her thighs.

Her breasts.

Never had she been like this at the club. Never had he seen anything like it.

The music got wilder and more frantic and her body writhed in rhythm to it.

Her hips rolling and bumping faster and faster, harder and harder, closer and closer to him. Her arms raised above her head, her mouth opened and her tongue started working in and out like a darting snake.

He was burning. He was aching with a hellish pain.

He couldn't stand it much longer.

Just when he was about to reach out for her in desperation, she moved closer. Her hips only inches from his face. She was quivering. Every muscle was vibrating wildly. Her skin was a rippling sea. The she slid down on his lap, squirmed against him and crushed her large, soft lips against his. He felt her tongue work into his mouth like a wiggling moist thing. It frantically pushed against his. Her body pressed harder. He felt wildly insane with burning passions. He worked his fingers against her yielding breasts. The flesh never seemed to end.

Then she started helping him off with his clothing.

After that it was one series of electric thrills after another, never stopping, never ending, and only getting wilder, more exciting, and more anxious.

She never seemed to want to stop.

But finally she did.

It was over, and she stood up, very business-like.

"You liked it?" she asked, in a still husky voice. "You liked me?"

He nodded. He didn't dare say a thing. His voice wouldn't work, he just knew it wouldn't.

She had been wonderful. Never had he felt anything so exciting, or thrilling, or more pleasurable. It had been worth a year's salary.

Then her hand went out.

"Twenty-five dollars...that's the price!" she snapped. "Twenty-five for tonight, and tomorrow it will only be twenty if you're still this good and if you are still interested."

She had him. He hadn't expected that. But she had him,

136

and she knew it. He paid. Gladly. And he would return. Oh, but how he would return!

She was going to be is private *Sizzle Girl!*

ೲFITTE THE TWENTY-SECONDೞ

So, this is something like a story, I suppose. A different look at the virginal seduction. In this case, we're dealing with a young man who discovered how one lady made the differ-ence in his life. And he would never forget her. (Don't even ask what the title has to do with the story. Even I'm not cer-tain about this one, other than it was used to inspire what followed!)

*SHE'S SOMETHING LIKE A DAME*ೞ

That's what all the men at the base called her. She was named Milly Rothington, a rather awkward name for a real sex-machine.

Her figure didn't know where to stop. And that was the way all the boys liked it.

Billy Sherman was a young man who had never had a woman before. And most of his friends realized that this was what made him so shy and backward. He had a very good brain and his looks were of the type that made woman jolly themselves up just at seeing him.

There was no reason in the world for him to be a virgin. *Yet there it was!*

"Look here, Billy, you're a grown man...and someone is likely to get the wrong idea about you...that is if you don't start breaking down some of these foolish ideas of yours!"

Billy just shook his head. Nervously he fingered his tie and didn't look directly into his friend's eyes.

Well, it was decided to get things moving, behind his

back, so to speak, in order to solve this problem for him.

Milly Rothington was summoned. She was paid in advance, and then introduced to Bill.

Billy didn't know her reputation; and since she had the most innocent look about her, never guessed what was happening.

"Hello, Billy!" she cooed shyly, looking up at him with large eyes wide open and honest.

"Hello…" he mumbled nervously.

She certainly is a pretty girl, he thought.

It was the occasion of the annual serviceman's ball, put on by the NCOs and officers for the enlisted men. Some came with girls, others didn't, since the place was well supplied with females from the local town.

But Milly had been chosen as Bill's date long before, and he was stuck with her.

Yet there was nothing better than being stuck with Milly. She had a figure that made all others look sick. The flesh bounced with every step she took. Her eyes flashed with every look she gave him.

"Like to dance?" he offered, not knowing what else to suggest, and not being able to think of anything to talk about.

Anyway, there's nothing like a dancing to bring a girl in close to you, he thought, hugging her full form to him.

It isn't to be taken that he was completely square-headed. He liked to dance close, and to neck heavily. But he had a strong rule against anything beyond passionate kissing.

She pressed close, eagerly.

He liked the feel of her, the delightful warm softness of her cheek.

"You're nice," she whispered in his ear, wiggling slightly against him.

"I like you too," he answered her compliment, squeezing her tighter.

They danced in silence for several moments, then she whispered, "Why don't we get out of here?"

He didn't know what to say at first. *Go where?*

"Where?" he asked after awhile.

"Oh," she shrugged, snuggling closer to him, "I know several places…."

"I…I don't know have any…car!"

"Don't worry about that; we can use mine!"

He thought it over for a long time, as they danced. It might be nice to run off…maybe go some place different—do something maybe a little different.

But what?

"Okay," he said, leading her off the dance floor. "They walked out into the cool night, and across the parking lot to a shiny new convertible.

"Wow!" he marveled. "What a rig!"

"You drive?"

"Sure do!"

"Then drive!" She handed him the keys.

He got behind the driver's seat and started the engine. It purred. "What a car! A real *bomb!*"

He glided the vehicle along the parked cars and onto the road. Then he let her out, flooring the pedal.

"Where to?" he inquired, turning toward the girl who had seated herself very close to him. She smiled up at him. Her lips were slightly parted.

"My place?" she shyly suggested, squeezing his arm affectionately.

That surprised him at first.

But after all, he thought, *she's safe with me!*

It wasn't far to where she lived, and her place was secluded and homey looking. He liked it.

"Your folks home?" he asked, as they got out of the car.

"Oh…" she choked slightly, then gained control of her slightly surprised vocal cords. "I thought you knew. I live alone!"

That one shocked him a little. Of course he had been prepared to discover that maybe her parents were out for the evening—but not that she lived alone.

"I didn't know—you're so young…"

She laughed. It was a bubbling sound that moved from her chest up through her throat in a low, husky nervousness. "I'm afraid I'm over twenty-one."

They walked up to the door of her apartment. She opened it. They went in.

It was a three-room affair. Nice. Warm. Cozy. She

turned on a dim light, then moved to the hi-fi in one corner of the living room.

"What kind of music do you like?" she asked, glancing back at him.

"Oh, anything!" he said, sitting down on the sofa. "Anything at all..."

He was a little confused and a little worried—concerned. *What kind of thing was he getting himself into? This had all the looks of a shack-up party—and that was definitely not the kind he was interested in...*

No! That wasn't it!

Sure, he'd like to get in bed with a girl—especially this one—but it was a matter of morals! The right thing and the wrong thing.

"Want a drink?" she asked, as music started filling the room with delightful rhythm and melody.

"Sure—I guess so!" He wasn't quite sure what he really wanted. He'd never had any kind of *drink*—liquor had been one thing he had always wanted to find out about but still afraid of trying. But suddenly he felt daring and curious.

What the hell!

"Any particular kind of drink?" she inquired moving toward the small kitchenette that was in reality only an extension of the living room.

"I...anything will do," he mumbled nervously. He felt suddenly excited, and at the same time guilty. Somewhere in the back of his brain he was afraid of himself, and what he might be tempted to do later this evening if the opportunity offered itself, which he was sure it would. And that was strangely unnerving.

A few moments later she came over and sat down beside him, handing him a tall glass with a punch-like drink in it.

"What is it?" he asked, mildly interested, since it didn't look anything like a drink—in the sense it must be!

"Punch—rum punch—hope you like it!" she smiled. Her eyes were sparkling brightly, as if they were holding back a comical secret.

He sipped this "punch," gulped slightly and then smiled. It was good tasting—a little on the...he didn't quite know the word for it—but quite excellent!

"Okay?" she asked grinning from ear to ear.

"Swell!" He let several more swallows follow the course of his throat and bounce from the hot core of his stomach, up into the upper reaches of his brain.

His blood pulsed. His skin heated.

His nerves tingled.

It was one hell of a pleasant drink!

He turned and looked at Milly. She had pulled her dress, or it had happened accidentally—which he doubted—above her knees. The smooth firm curves of her legs were exposed. They were beautiful. He was tempted to reach out and touch them. But he didn't dare.

Where the hell were all these crazy thoughts coming from?

One look at those wide, innocent blue eyes should tell him that this was a *nice* girl! Her mouth was delightfully moist, full and velvety looking.

He shook his head. He was getting all kinds of weird thoughts. *Crazy, insane thoughts and ideas!*

Her hand was idly caressing her calf, and he abruptly found himself wanting her more than anything in the world. He wanted to feel the soft, silky texture of their creamy skin.

Her fingers caught on the edge of her skirt, and "accidentally" raised the cloth further.

He felt eager sweat move down his body. Nervously he gulped some more of the punch, and the warming liquid burned through him.

"You been in the service long?" she asked, fingering a button on the top of her white blouse. It came unlatched.

"I...I—no! Just about five months...or so!" he muttered in a low, husky voice.

Her skirt was rising further upwards.

"You like...me?"

Her fingers circled on his thigh, her eyes following movement.

There was a long silence, then she leaned toward him, and whispered softly. "Kiss me."

He didn't have much to say about the matter—really. She came into his arms, and crushed herself against his chest. He could feel the pressure of her. The heating of her heart pounded eagerly. Her lips moved on his, moist and open, anxious and warm.

They parted after a long, searching excitement that had winded them.

"Make love to me!" she pleaded in an almost demanding voice. "Yes, do that!"

She raised her blouse over her head, and pulled it off. She had only a bra on underneath. Blood was throbbing at his temples just from watching the delightful display.

She was breathing heavily. "Take me, honey, I'm all your's."

He was burning with desire for her. His head felt oddly fuzzy. He couldn't think straight.

"Stop!" he demanded, forcing her away from him. "Stop right now!"

She looked at him in shock. Her face contorted savagely. She stood. Then in a fury of action she raised her skirt deliberately higher.

A short-circuit took place somewhere in his driving motivational centers.

"What's wrong, little boy?" she questioned in a nasty voice. "Don't you like girls?"

"You—" he cried, standing and starting for the door.

She got there before him.

"What's wrong with you—you a little prude—sissy boy?" she questioned.

It was all he could do to control himself. The drink had fired every nerve in him and she was burning, liquid fire.

God, how he wanted her! his mind cried in torment, as he looked at her perfect, bewitching form. Never had he seen such perfection; such sensual beauty and excitement.

The burn tormented him until he was dizzy.

She laughed tauntingly. "I knew you wanted me...I know you want me! You're just afraid! That it?"

He nodded foolishly. He wanted to get out and run, and get away from this devilish temptress. But he couldn't even move from where he was. He was burning all over. His mind was fuzzed.

"What are you afraid of?" she demanded, sliding her arms around his neck, and moving closer to him. Her lips

143

brushed his cheek, slipping around toward his ear. Everything about her was pure silk. Full, firm, silk. "I want to be loved—I know you'll like it—you will, believe me! Oh, how you will."

Her lips moved lightly on his ear lobe. It felt delightfully wonderful; exciting.

Suddenly he didn't care any more. Suddenly, for the first time in his life, he realized he wanted to live life and enjoy the pleasures of being a man. Who knew what tomorrow might bring; then it might be too late. He would hate dying a virgin.

She was here in his arms, wanting to be loved. There was no *asking* involved. No awkward building up on his part—no chance of being turned down!

Here she was!

Begging him! Wanting him.

And he realized that it had been more his fear of being turned down, or making the wrong move, or having the girl think he was inexperienced.

All those things had been part of his fear of sex. Now they didn't count here. She was begging to be taken— wanting him to love her.

The rest would be easy.

He followed her into the bedroom to take her wonder loving body, and discover what it was like to totally possess a lovely, wonderful woman.

Later, of course, his friends never told him the truth about how she had been hired to seduce him. Strangely enough he never saw the lady again. But it didn't matter. For now he was a man on the make! He was too busy searching out new adventures, with other wonderful young ladies, willing to share night hours with an experience young man.

She had been something more than just a dame, she'd been a wonderful first experience and he would never forget her. For she had taught him that he was desirable and the ladies that followed proved her right on!

৩FITTE THE TWENTY-THIRD৶

Some women will do anything to seduce a man. And some men can be pretty quickly frightened off a hot broad when a huge giant comes along, claiming she was off limits. But this singing bird was a hot canary who would stop at nothing to possess him.

*THE CAT AND THE CANARY*৶

It was near closing time when the girl, all smiles, curves, and warmth, approached him saying she was applying for the job as a vocalist. One look at her and he felt as if he'd been grabbed where it felt the most sensitive. Like Wow! And How! The moment he saw her, a *dizzy* floating sensation plastered him against the ceiling. At least that's the way it felt.

Maybe it was the drinks.

He didn't know.

But it was sex at first sight!

A light airy excitement that moved from his guts and rippled around his nervous system numbed his brain to nothingness.

"My name's Jackie..." she murmured. "You Jim the Horn?" she asked.

"Sure thing, baby!"

Her body was pushing out so wildly against the tight fitting red dress that he didn't know for sure which would win: the dress or her!

The dip at the top was cut so low that it couldn't get any

lower and still be decent.

She was speaking about how anxious she was to work with his group. He hardly heard a word; didn't care what she said. It was such a thrill just staring at this lush lovely.

She had the blondest hair he had ever seen. He wondered if it could really be real.

Impossible!

"Like Daddy, blow me a chorus on *Lazy River*!" she murmured in such a low husky voice that he wasn't sure if she weren't somehow having her jollies right then and there.

"Like crazy!" he exclaimed, nodding to Benny, the piano man, and putting his trumpet to his lips. After a wild intro of eight bars, he nodded to the girl to start blowing.

Then his notes went flat with a high-pitched screech, as she gave her body such a wiggle that the wonders on her chest did a rock n' roll. His eyes just flipped in time with their juggling. He didn't hear the lovely quality of her voice; he was blinded death by her bobbin' boobs.

Then that vibrant, way-down voice of hers filled the room in a real way out sorta way and actually penetrated his brain. What a voice!

Well, she was hired that moment. For anything she wanted, in fact!

"Like chick!" he said after she was finished, moving up to her and running his arm around her waist, squeezing her seductively, "Crazy!" He turned her toward the bar. "Come on, baby, have a tall cool one."

Seated on the tall stool, she moved close to him, pressing her hip against his, and they sat quietly for a while, both enjoying the warm, intimate contact.

When the drinks were served she wiggled even nearer.

She turned toward him and all the tropical fires lighted her eyes and face. Her full, silky red lips opened into just about the sexiest grin he had ever seen.

"Like, are you going to use me?" she asked, raising the drink to her mouth.

"Well...I..." he tried to make his voice seem business-like, but it was hard under the influence of those rising and falling valuables on her chest. "Well, tell you what, I'll give you a week's trial! And see how things work out!"

146

"Oh...gosh, thanks!" she cried, moving closer and moving her lips against his.

He flipped.

Right then and there.

It was the most excited kiss he had ever had. The silkiest and hottest lips he had ever felt.

Then a huge hand gripped his shoulder and spun him around, almost flipping him off the bar stool. A steel fist smashed into his face, and another into his stomach.

"Lay off this canary!" a deep, man's voice vibrated out of the air around him.

He felt sick.

Terribly sick.

"Hands off. You let her sing. But you leave her alone!" Another hammer-like blow smashed into the side of his head, and he fell to the floor, blackness pushing down upon him.

The next thing he remembered was a dim, tiny light coming into focus far away and directly in front of him. It was like he was speeding through a dark tunnel; the white dot kept getting bigger and bigger. It weaved in front of his eyes, then finally burst into reality

He was in his dressing room. Benny, his piano man, was standing over him.

"You all right, boss?" the man asked.

"Don't know..." he moaned, slowly rising. "What hit me?"

"The girl's boyfriend, I guess." Benny grinned despite himself. "Boy, what a man. A giant. Wouldn't want to tangle with him, ever."

It took Jim several hours to get back to normal.

Luckily his lip hadn't been hurt too badly, and he was able to blow the next night.

But what surprised everybody was when the girl turned up for work...*alone!* She acted as if nothing had happened. Went over like an atomic bomb with the audience.

When she was finished for the night, and the last set was being played by the combo, she sat at the bar looking at him for a long time. She smiled every time their eyes met; and afterwards when the club closed, she walked over to where he was collecting some of the music.

"Honey," she whispered softly, her lips only inches from his ear. "Isn't there something I can...I mean I feel horrible about this last night. I feel terrible...just terrible!"

He turned toward her. She was so very near. He could smell the excitement of her perfume as it scented the air around them. Her breathing seemed unnaturally heavy. Her lips were moistly pink. "I...I mean I feel sorry about it..." she stammered.

The words held promise of something else. They said more completely what she was thinking and wanting, than if she had come right and said she wanted to be taken by him.

He shook himself.

He didn't want to get wound up with that boyfriend of hers again. The guy was a savage and would probably put him in the hospital for a month. Now way! *That's all he needed.*

Next time he might not be in any condition to blow anything at all.

He ignored her obvious offer.

The next night she made the same offer, silent and completely suggestive.

He still didn't want to get involved with any trouble he couldn't handle. And he knew damn well he couldn't handle that boyfriend of hers.

But when her friend didn't turn up after two weeks of continuous effort on her part to become friendlier, he couldn't resist any longer.

It was on the eve of her third week at the club that he decided to take her on, if she pulled her seductive tricks on him again.

But this time, when the show was over, she wasn't anywhere to be found.

She had disappeared.

She wasn't anywhere in the club.

Regretfully, he drove to his apartment in West Los Angeles, parked his car in the garage, and went up to his room.

The lights were on.

He could see a yellow glow through the crack between the bottom of the door and the floor.

148

He hadn't left them on; he was sure of that! He opened the door.

Stopped short.

Shocked. He couldn't believe his eyes. He couldn't think of anything to say. He couldn't even think.

Then sudden fear moved through him.

"Hi," Jackie said, smiling brightly, walking across the room. Her hips swung delightfully. Her legs moved cat-like. Her breasts bobbed and bounced.

"I thought you weren't coming home." she added as she stopped in front of him. "You took so long…"

She stood there, her hips pushed forward slightly, her body balanced more on one leg than the other. Her breasts pointed outwards through the low-cut gown she was wearing.

"I…I…" He couldn't talk. He was afraid. He was abruptly terrified that her boy friend would show up and find her there in his apartment.

He couldn't do anything. The terror worked through him.

Then frantic action followed. He turned and closed the door. His breathing was a pounding thing inside him. Sweat was working all over his body.

"What the hell are you doing here?" he cried, running across the room to the windows. He pulled the blinds, and then turned toward her. He was still breathing hard, and not only from fear, or the frantic running around, but also a little because of her. And that hot body.

She was the hottest thing he had ever seen.

And there wasn't a woman in the world that he wanted more.

"Don't be silly," she cooed, leaning back against the door and looking across the room at him. "What do you think?"

Laughter bubbled over her, shaking every curve, every cone and valley of her figure.

*"You…*look so…terrified. I won't bite!" she gasped between giggles.

"Well…I…" He had never felt so weak, or helpless, or silly. His legs were quivering.

149

"Oh, baby...come on...all I want is you and me to have some fun together. Don't worry about anything else..." she rasped through heated vocal cords. She reached around her back, and then there was the sound of a zipper.

The dress fell to the floor around her feet. She stepped out of the circle of cloth and moved toward him. She was smiling. She was completely naked.

She came into his arms, and he forgot his terror, his trembling fear. He forgot everything in her arms.

That body writhed around him until he was aware of nothing else but that burning passion it created and expressed.

Afterwards she left.

The next night she was in his dressing room when the placed had closed. They repeated their actions of the evening before. Then it happened.

Just like that. Without any warning. The door opened to his room, and in walked a giant of a man.

The girl was completely nude, locked in his arms. He felt a ripple of terror run through her body, vibrating her breasts. He turned and saw the huge man standing in the middle of the room, looking at them.

"I told you, mister, if you..." the man bellowed stepping toward them.

Jim felt terror take control of him.

This was it, and he wanted to run, or shrivel into nothingness.

"Stop!" he screamed, as a hand was laid on his shoulder.

The man stopped.

That surprised him.

"At least tell me why?" he cried, starting to slowly rise. Then without any warning he rammed his fist into the man's stomach, then another blow at his lowered chin.

The man crumpled to the floor. Not another sound issued from him.

Jim couldn't believe it.

It couldn't be that easy. It was impossible that it could be that easy.

"Who is he?" he asked Jackie.

Her eyes were contracted in horror, and surprise.

150

"How did you do it?" she cried.

"I don't know!"

"He's...he's an old friend..." she sat down, and her face smiled brightly. "Oh, daddy what a man you are..."

"You mean you don't mind—I mean..." He hadn't been quite sure what her reaction. He was afraid that she liked the man or so thing.

But then...

"Oh, I never thought there would be a man who could do what you just did," she screamed in delight, leaping toward him. Her arms ran around neck, and she pressed herself against him.

"Oh, my hero!" she cried.

He was almost glad.

He was still shaking from fear. *What if the guy came to?*

He pushed her away; a bit terrified of what was taking place.

"We gotta get out of here, fast! Before he comes to!" he said frantically.

"Oh, don't be silly. What can he do to you?" she sighed, kissing him anxiously.

"For God's sake!" he screamed, looking at those gigantic arms on the other man. He hated to think what the man could do.

"Oh, forget *him!*" she whispered huskily. "Just take me home. He won't bother you."

"What the hell do you mean?"

"He's my brother...we always pull this," she sighed, pushing him out the door, into the darkened night club. "After all, a girl doesn't want to think a man is just taking her for pure kicks. Anybody who will fight for a girl...*must care!*"

His head spun.

He couldn't believe his ears.

But...what the hell! he thought as they walked across the silent room. *She might be a nut...and crazy...and that blasted beating he had taken...nut hell!*

He looked at her for a long time, and the lust, desire, longing just surged through him like a fantastic forest fire.

"You're some cat!" she laughed in delight, taking his hand in hers.

"And you're some canary!" he muttered, still stunned as they left her brother on the floor in his dressing room.

She might be crazy, a real nut, but one hell of a singing, swinging bird with not only a lovely voice and fantastic body, she had what it took to blow his horn any time, night or day. From then on the would be known as the ...

WILD CAT AND THE SINGIN' CANARY!

Of course he would have to pay her more, considering she'd be top billing. But...

She was worth it!
And how!

ℬFITTE THE TWENTY-FOURTH℞

When a girl resists, beware, she could be after more than you might expect. This bit of fluff offers some indirect answers about how…

TO HUSTLE A HUSTLER℞

It was Sunday, and Dale was lounging on the hotel porch when the blonde walked out from the lobby, looking like something from a movie set. Her body was decked out in a tight-fitting red dress that exposed too much of her thrusting breasts to give her any appearance of class.

Dale checked that fact mentally and then sat up, dropping his legs to the porch. His eyes went over her figure, making it as obvious as possible.

It had been several nights since he'd bedded down with a woman, and months since one like this had crossed his path. She radiated sex from every pore.

"Hello," he greeted, smiling.

The blonde turned large brown eyes in his direction, appraising him. They hesitated at his wrinkled slacks and T-shirt.

"My name's Dale Gordon," he began, standing and moving to her. He couldn't keep his eyes off that lush figure.

"So?" she inquired in a low, rich voice. She turned her attention to the beach in front of the hotel.

"Well, I thought maybe—"

"You're wasting your time, Mr. Gordon," she snapped, stepping away, walking down toward the beach. Her hips wiggled provocatively.

That was enough to convince him.

One way or another, Dale promised himself, he'd con her into a bed-party.

Dale didn't see her again until that evening at the dining room. She was sitting at a table alone, eating pork chops. A cocktail, half drained, was beside her plate.

After a moment's hesitation, Dale stepped over to her table, smiling. "Hello, again."

Her eyes looked up coldly, but she didn't say anything.

"Mind if I join you?"

"There're other tables," she pointed out.

"None as attractively decorated," he announced, letting his eyes fall to the low cut of her neckline, where two spheres of creamy flesh bulged.

Without waiting for an objection, Dale sat opposite her. He looked boldly into the woman's eyes, communicating silently.

"You're a little pushy—aren't you, Mr. Gordon?"

"Well, I made an impression after all. You remember my name."

She laughed, throatily. "Let's say you've made an impression."

Silence settled over them. Several times she started to say something, and then stopped short.

The waiter came, and Dale ordered T-bone steak and a double martini.

"Will you have another cocktail?" he offered the blonde.

Her eyes leveled with his. "You sure you want to waste your money?"

"I have more than enough—might as well take me for a ride," he laughed.

A flicker of interest sparked her eyes as she nodded.

The waiter left and the blonde asked: "You vacationing?"

"More or less. Work in Industrial Steel."

"Oh?" The question was a polite probe.

Dale shrugged. "It pays well, and my company gets big governmental contracts."

The cocktails came as he asked: "I take it you're on a

vacation, too."

Her smile was the only answer.

By the time food had arrived and the drinks were re-freshed, he learned her name was Ruth Bennings. Beyond that, she told nothing about herself. After the meal they sat smoking and finishing off the last drink. Dale's head was dizzily affected by the martinis, and he imagined the woman was feeling the same way by now. She had warmed up, be-coming friendly, yet quietly reserved.

"You wouldn't consider a walk along the beach, would you?" he suggested.

"What did you have in mind?" she inquired.

"A walk—what else?" It was a lie, and she knew it, but he didn't care much any more. Several points had been al-ready made, and he wasn't in any hurry now to rush off into the bedroom.

"Some men get the idea that a woman who takes a walk with them on a lonely beach might do more."

"You're an attractive woman, Ruth," he admitted. "Any man would want to make a pass at you."

She smiled, but revealed no other reaction to his words. A little later they left, walking out into the dark night.

The moon was only in the first quarter and hidden be-hind dark clouds. As they walked along the beach, the sound of waves hitting the sands was a soft murmur in the back-ground. The air was chilled, moving lightly against them.

Ruth walked close to him and every few moments her hip and thigh brushed his like an electric caress. They hadn't said anything for a long time, and he couldn't help wonder-ing if her thoughts were running the same course as his own. Each touch of her leg and hip sent fire through him, pushing the desire to an almost uncontrollable stage. The wanting to sweep her into his arms finally brought him to a stop in front of her.

Before she could resist, Dale pulled her against him, kissing her.

The impact of her nearness, the supple feel of her volup-tuous body, ripped at the passion that had been boiling in him all day.

She blended against him, her lips parted hesitantly and

155

then she writhed wildly, pushing her moist tongue deep into his mouth.

After a long moment they drew apart.

"You shouldn't—have...done that," she stammered, eyes blazing into his.

"Why?"

"You know. I said I didn't want anything like this."

Dale laughed, staring down at her. "Don't tell me the thought hadn't entered your mind before this."

"It had," she admitted.

"So?"

"I warn you—you might be sorry—very sorry."

"What's there to be sorry about?" Dale demanded, pulling her into his arms.

She struggled free, her expression strangely veiled. "You asked for it."

Ruth slipped out of her dress a moment after they closed the door to his hotel room. She stood boldly before him, her breasts cupped upwards by a half bra which exposed the pink centers.

"I just hope you don't regret what you started," she announced, unclasping the bra and dropping it on top of her dress on the floor.

Heat dried his throat as he reached for her. His lips buried into the silken cream of her throat and she brazenly pressed her hips against his.

Lifting her in his arms, he went to the bed. They folded tightly together, locking in a savage embrace, his hand cupping one breast as she moved under him. It was like holding down a tigress. She whipped from side to side, clawing, biting, straining.

His lips slid over her body, voluptuously kissing its velvet flesh. Then as the madness slashed at his nerves, he reached for her hips.

The next moments thrashed out the last straining pleasure.

Dale rolled away from her, lying on his back, bathed in the wonderful glowing aftermath of exhaustion. His back felt as if it had been stripped raw of flesh. Her nails had cut raggedly at him during those wildly delicious last seconds.

156

How long he lay there before she reached for him, he didn't know. There was a vague feeling that he'd fallen asleep for a short time.

Her hands awakened the desire as they searched over him, and then they were starting all over again, their bodies laced violently together until exhaustion dropped him back once more, this time to fold sleep over all awareness.

When he awoke the sun was shining across his eyes. He sat up, looking for Ruth.

A quick search of the room revealed that she had left; and revealed one hell of a lot more.

His clothing was piled in the middle of the room, the pockets turned inside out. His wallet was on the floor, opened.

On the mirror, red smeared a short, curt message:

"You bastard— and not a damned dime!"

After a startled moment, Dale doubled over, laughter convulsing him. Finally he stood, starting to gather up his clothing. Then looked at his wrist watch. It was 8:45.

Ten minutes later he was in the hotel kitchen, frantically cleaning the pile of dishes which had gotten a head start on him. But he was whistling happily all the time.

ഔFITTE THE TWENTY-FIFTH☞

Some say "The Devil made me do it." Well, in this case, we might say that sometimes the end results are stranger than Hell itself. When playboy Bill met hot Sherry it was time for Heaven & Hell to mate. Well, let's say he was about to become the lover of...

SATAN'S MISTRESS☞

"Sherry's one girl even you can't get," Bill Belmont told him.

Carl Gordon looked at the nude picture of the woman, laughed: "With that body—you kidding?"

The photographer shrugged:

"She's one of those expensive virgins. She models, but that's all."

Carl looked at the picture again.

The woman had long black hair which went down to her shoulders. Her body was built so that it was a walking man-trap. She had curves that most men dreamed about. Her breasts were large, firm and self-supporting, if the photo didn't lie. Their centers were rigid and erect, temptingly inviting. The flat expanse of her stomach was supported by wide circular hips which blended downward to thick, beefy thighs.

"Come on, Bill, tell me the truth. You've been getting to her and don't want the competition cutting into your territory."

"No, to be frank," the man admitted sadly. "Don't think

158

I haven't tried. The day I took this her out—last week—I suggested a cocktail. Her answer was embarrassingly pointed. "You're wasting your time. Drunk or sober—sorry!"

Carl smiled cockily, looked proudly at himself in the large mirror on the far wall, taking in the even, finely hand-some features of his manly face and then letting his eyes cover the full length of his lean six-foot frame before turning his attention to his host.

"How about introducing us?"

Bill just frowned and shrugged. "You're wasting your time, Carl. I've heard the same story from other guys."

"There's a price for every girl. She intrigues me. More than intrigues me—desires are way, way up. It's a challenge! All you gotta do is find which button to push. Hell, they'll fly into bed. Believe me—I know, from experience!"

The photographer shook his head. "Sure, you have the looks, the money and the charm. But you're going to meet your match with Sherry MacManners. She just won't go. But if you're willing to blow a wad on her account, I wouldn't be the guy to stop you."

"Bet you a steak dinner I make the point!"

After a short moment to consider, Bill nodded.

* * * * * * *

The woman that sat next to Carl, in the car, was a dream. She was even more beautiful and desirable in the flesh. Color did things for her. The photograph hadn't revealed the white cream of her skin, or the flawless texture of its silky smooth-ness. It didn't even hint at the gleaming blue sparkle in her large eyes or the full redness of her wide, velvet lips.

She was dressed in a revealing gown which cut away at the front and back. The front advertised two thrusting orbs of supple flesh, evenly separated to give a delightful view of the valley between. The back cut inviting the desire to caress the even smoothness of naked flesh.

It was hard to think this was a woman that went out of her way to play the cool, cold virgin-chick. Everything about her screamed experience with men.

"I'm certainly glad you let me take you out," Carl told her. "I was afraid you wouldn't go along with this idea of a blind date."

Sherry smiled and touched his arm with long, tapered fingers. "I've heard about you, so you might say I more or less know you—from reputation."

The corners of her lips moved upwards, revealing gleaming even white teeth. The implication was surprising, because he would have thought the idea of his reputation with women would have shied her away.

"I've heard a lot about you," he admitted, directing the car into the parking lot of the *Iron Castle Steak House*.

A few minutes later they were sitting at a small table, sipping cocktails. Her dark eyes were staring deep into his.

"What did you hear about me?" she inquired.

"Well, do you want honesty or flattery?"

"There shouldn't be any difference, if you're a gentleman.

Carl laughed and then finished his martini. "Well, I heard you're quite a woman."

"And that I don't play around? she pushed, her gaze leveled on his.

"Let's say that I'd heard you're a respectable woman."

For a moment her face revealed no reaction, then a light twinkle flared and she subtly smiled. "I like that, Carl. I like that a lot."

They ordered steaks, had after-dinner cocktails and then went across town to a small hotel that had a cocktail lounge that featured dancing. They settled into a booth on the far side of the lounge, away from the dance floor, ordered cocktails, held hands in a warm, friendly way and waited for the drinks to come.

"Tell me something about yourself, Sherry," Carl suggested.

"Well, I'm a working girl, trying to get into a solid career as a model and maybe into acting. I guess I'm no different from other women my age."

"You're different, believe me. I've seen a lot and you're quite different!"

"Well, thank you—I hope that means you like me."

160

"Let's say I'll reserve that until later." He intimately squeezed her fingers. Sherry frowned, reaction showed.

The cocktails came, sipped them, and a little later lie suggested a dance.

The rhythm of her body against his stimulated all the male hormones to wild madness. Her form was soft, yielding suppleness against him. Her hips moved lightly, but had an intimate, suggestive quality that cried for him to reach around and press her closer to him. The scent of her perfume sent sensual messages to his brain centers; but, beyond that, there was no other intimacy or implications exchanged. They danced for a little while, returned to their table arid sipped martinis.

Again he probed her for information about her interests and past, and learned that she had been raised in New York, come out West when she was nineteen and worked in an office until having gotten into modeling. Now she made her full living letting photographers take pictures of her for magazines.

"What do you do for social...intercourse?

She laughed throatily at that, wagged her finger playfully at him, as if he had said something naughty and shouldn't have.

"I mean...any men in your life?" he inquired innocently.

"That depends on what you mean by men. I've had male friends."

But she wouldn't go into any details beyond that. It was while they were sitting in front of her apartment in the car that he learned a very important fact about her. They were talking about the latest satellite which the U. S. had put up when she burst out with such an angry flow of words that he was left stunned almost to disbelief.

"Scientists! They should be damned to hell! They bring nothing to us but trouble. Damn them! Can't they leave things alone? If it weren't for them, things would have been perfect—perfect! But they came along and ruined everything. That's the trouble with the world. Sinful! Sinful with science! We were fine until then!" Then she suddenly broke off, as if she'd said too much.

Sherry's face was flushed and her eyes downcast. For a

161

long time she was breathing hard and then she gained control and turned, saying: "I think I'd better go on in."

"Wait a minute—what did you mean? We were fine until then!"

"Nothing—nothing at all!" When they arrived at her doorstep, she turned, her face now completely expressionless.

"It's been nice, Carl. Thanks." She started unlocking her door.

"How about a nightcap?" he suggested.

"No, Carl. If you asked around, you should know that I—well, you'd be wasting your time. If that's what you asked me out for—then I'm sorry for you." She stared coldly into his eyes.

"No. No—not at all. That's not what I meant. Really. Just that I...well, I just didn't want the evening to end, that's all." he reached for her, trying to draw her body close to his.

She struggled free, her eyes fiery. "Don't, Carl. I can't let you do that to me." Her eyes instinctively looked up toward the sky, at the moon which was at quarter

He followed her gaze, a strange feeling settling over him, When he looked back to where she'd been standing, she was gone, the door closed.

For a long time he stood there, dazed, let-down, but strangely intrigued.

Once more he looked up at the moon. What had that instinctive glance meant? Nothing? Or something all important. "I can't let you do that to me." Not that she didn't want him to but couldn't let him.

Slowly he turned and walked down the steps to his car. All the way home he puzzled over her words. Taken by themselves, they meant little. But put together, he couldn't help thinking they might hold the clue to her sexual coldness. Not that he had expected to really make his point the first night—but at least he should have gotten a first-base kiss. Her outburst against science, her looking at the moon. What did they mean?

The next day he called a friend of his who ran a private detective agency.

"Dale, I want you to look into the background and full

activities of a woman named Sherry MacManners. Watch her every move for a month."

"It'll cost," his friend assured him.

"So—I have to find out something about her. Get as many men as necessary on the job. I have money to burn, so you might as well make a little of it."

In the next weeks he took Sherry out a couple of times, just to make it look good. Each tune everything went well as long as he didn't try to make a pass at her. Once he brought up the subject of sexual philosophy, and undertones of darkness shadowed her face.

She said: "There's a right place for everything." Then, later, a deeper hint as to her attitude about such things was revealed. "In the Dark Ages they believed—rather some believed—that sexual freedom should be allowed—there were sects that worshipped the Devil and had banquets in which wild orgies were enjoyed by all." The nervous laugh which followed that statement caused a shiver to tremble down his spine.

It was exactly one month and a day before he got his report from the detective agency.

The background was unimportant. What jarred meaning into the whole report—and the many hints which she had suggested to him—was a statement that she belonged to a secret cult which worshipped the Devil. They called themselves the *Satanic Cult of Sensual Studies*. At this point the report read:

"The Cult meets at the full moon at a huge house on Mable Street, address below, and they hold what they called Satan Rites. All the members we could learn about are unmarried and have reputations as being ultra moralistic in their associations with outside people."

At the bottom of the message there was a handwritten note from Dale:

"What you getting into? I did a little investigating on my own on the Cult and their beliefs. How about letting me in on it? I take it you're interested in getting at the Sherry MacManners girl. Call me if you get into the 'Club'."

That afternoon, Carl drove out to the address on Mable Street.

The building was a large, white house with two stories. It must have been built at the turn of the century, but was well kept. When he went up to it, knocking on the door, a little peep-hole opened and a voice asked:

"What is it you want?"

"I heard about this place. That there's a…well…club that meets here and I'm interested in it."

"Sorry—you must have wrong information," The little peep hole slammed shut.

He knocked several times, but received no answer.

Disgusted, Carl returned to his car and sat there for a long time, trying to decide what next to do. One way or another he was going to have Sherry.

When he drove home he called her, made a date for the next night.

That evening, in bed, sleep was long in coming, and when it did finally arrive, it was filled with dreams. Dreams which horrified him.

He was in a dark room, Silence surrounding him. Then he heard a voice call out. "Carl—Carl. You want to be one of us you want to be one of us!"

Then the form of the Devil exploded into being before his eyes. The satanic image grinned, its horns flaming. "You want to become one of us. Then you must have Sherry MacManners—she is yours!"

The Devil changed form, its body slowly filling out into a feminine shape. And then suddenly it was Sherry, naked, inviting, and seductive. She reached her arms out for him, drawing herself tightly against his body; writhing, as their lips met. Then she slipped away from him laughing. When he ran after her she would continue to be just out of reach, until at last he awoke in bed, sweat covering his body.

That evening, when he went to pick Sherry up at her apartment, into which she had never allowed him to enter, he determined that once and for all he was going to push through her resistance and come right out and reveal his knowledge of her membership in the Satanic Cult

When he first met her that evening he tried to approach the subject, but something stopped him, something in the expression on Sherry's face.

164

It wasn't until late in the evening that the conversation finally drifted in the right direction. They were, as they had been many times in the past, sitting in the car, outside her apartment.

He had placed an arm around her shoulder and she was leaning close, more intimate than ever before.

"Sherry," he managed, "I learned about the house on Mable Street."

The woman tensed against him, her breath sucked in, and then after an instant pause she seemed to have gained control.

"What are you talking about?" she inquired, puzzled.

"The moon and the Devil and love. That's what I'm talking about. I learned about the Satanic Cult."

A flicker of terror and surprise shadowed her face. "What are you...you're kidding?"

"No—how about it? I'm interested," he pushed.

Now her lips spread into a warming smile. "Are you serious about that?"

"Serious."

"Why?"

For a moment he considered that question, instinctively realizing it to be loaded. Impulse almost caused him to tell the truth, then he quickly told her:

"Because I learned to admire your mind—everything about you. I like you one hell of a lot. I'll admit that when I saw your photograph for the first time there were mere animal hungers pushing me. But now that I've gotten to know you—well, I'm quite interested in knowing more—more about those things you are interested in. What's this cult have? Why do you go to it?"

A murmur of pleasure sounded from her throat. She looked dreamily into his eyes. "Oh, Carl—I was hoping that was the reason you were interested. But how did you find out?"

"My methods. Let's just say I found out. That's all." He squeezed her closer, sure that now she would give in for a kiss. But she stiffened, gently pushing him away.

"No, Carl. No. You surely know now the reasons why I can't do anything like that, now." She smiled and patted his cheek.

"How about the club? Can't I—"

"Of course, darling," she purred, smiling. "Of course. Next week—the moon will be full, then, the meeting takes place there at the House—and I'll take you there—and you will see why I am a part of it—and you will learn a lot about me. Pick me up at six-thirty and we will go out to dinner— and afterwards we'll go to the house."

He started to get out of the car but she motioned him to forget it. When she had disappeared into her apartment, Carl started the car, a pleased grin spreading across his face.

It wouldn't he long now, he thought happily. Then on second thought he realized that there wasn't any sure promise of anything other than a meeting. Well, in a week he'd know.

* * * * * * *

By the time they had finished their after-dinner cocktails it was well past nine and Sherry told him they had better leave for the House.

The week had been hard on him, every night filled with dreams of chasing Sherry through dark corridors, but never getting her.

When they arrived at the House, the place looked dark and empty, but the moment the door opened, Carl realized that it was far from empty.

There was a dim light in the hallway which created a semi-gloom that folded around them as the door closed. The tall, thin man who had answered Sherry's knock silently motioned them forward into a huge living room.

Half a dozen people were sitting in the middle of the bare room. The only object in the room was a small platform in front of a curtained doorway. Everyone was silent, waiting, their eyes frozen to the curtain.

Sherry had told him to remain quiet and do exactly what she did.

They sat down and waited.

Several other couples came after them during the next twenty minutes. Music softly filled the room and the lights dimmed almost to blackness.

Carl reached a hand for Sherry's but when he contacted hers she pushed it way.

All he could hear was the music and the soft breathing of the people around him. A nervousness caused laughter to threaten to take control of him.

Surely these people couldn't be taking it all this seriously, he thought, looking around the at the half glazed faces which were mere shadows in the semi-darkness.

Then suddenly the dark curtain parted and a tall, regal man stepped out. He was dressed in a business suit and cape around his large shoulders.

"Greetings, Oh fellow worshippers," he cried in a low, bass voice.

"Greetings," everybody murmured back.

"Is everybody living a good life?"

"Yes."

"Are we ready for the night's activities?"

"Yes," they cried.

"Then think, Oh men of Worship—think of the Devil's promise of pleasure without punishment—think of Satan's all embracing desire to fold the multitudes into his charmed circle so they can enjoy the fires of passion, so they can experience the full pleasure of their bodies.

"There is one among us who is a stranger—who wishes to become one of the Inner Circle. That Stranger will stand and step forward." It was some time before Carl realized that the man was talking to him. Then a sense of panic overcame him. What if he laughed? What if he couldn't restrain all urge to let the comic side of what was taking place overwhelm him?

"Stranger—stand and step forward, so all can see you."

Carl slowly stood, forced his feet to move forward.

When he was standing before the tall man, he suddenly became aware of a strange odor that attacked his nostrils. For an instant, fear iced over his spine Then he felt a sickening dizziness cloud his vision.

He tried to look at the man, but couldn't.

Then he felt hands reach for him and lift him forward.

Black curtains parted and then he was standing in a

small room, opposite a golden altar on which stood an urn from which purple fumes were coming.

Carl was aware of being alone in the room, not knowing what to do, or what was expected of him.

He was just about to turn and leave, disgusted, when a dizziness caused him to stagger forward, stumble. He was falling into a deep pit, falling, falling into darkness.

"Get up, Oh man that would become one with myself," a satanic voice ordered.

Carl tried to clear the dreamy fuzziness from his brain.

He struggled to his feet, and found himself gazing into the features of Satan.

A long, powerful nose, red-tipped, arched eyebrows, a pointed beard, thick, huge lips, fury filled evil crimson eyes glared almost inches from his own face.

If this wasn't the Devil, it was a wildly horrifying image of what It should look like.

And behind this image was what appeared to be the shadow of a long fork-tipped tail swishing back and forth into the endless distance. The illusion was strangely real, too real.

Terror choked up through him, mingled with surprise and a light nausea. He was seeing things. Surely seeing things. Or dreaming. That was it.

"I am Satan," the evil creature said, "and I am here to enter you into my Kingdom of Worship. From this day on you will never be able to enjoy physical union except with members of our Inner Circle. With them you will have all the pleasures of ecstasy—but not from the others in the outside world."

This was, of course, surely nothing but a man made-up to appear Satanic. His head was fashioned in the realist form of what was generally accepted to be Satan! Most impressive; and surely some stunt to impress new members of this cult into believing whatever they needed to believe to release natural sexual urges that had been locked up tight in the cages of their prudish minds.

This demon creature touched his head and blinding light shot over his body, numbing it, sending soft tingling sensations through every nerve.

168

Every inch of his body felt as if it had been bathed in electric fire. His brain was throbbing wildly. He felt as if he were spinning through a dark endless tunnel. Finally lights burst into being with a series of blinding flashes. Stars fluttered, popped, exploded in multicolored burst.

Then suddenly he was in blackness again. He couldn't have been unconscious for long. The sound of Sherry's voice awakened him and he looked up into her eyes.

She smiled, helping him to stand.

"What happened?" he questioned in the classical way of all stunned and dazed people.

"You are now truly one with us. Follow me," she murmured, leading him through a small door and then down a hallway. In moments they walked into a bedroom and she closed the door behind him.

"Oh, Carl, you don't know how happy I am that you wanted to join us—I've was desperate to know what it could be like with you—I've really wanted to know—but I guess you understand why I couldn't before now."

"What are you talking about?" his mind was clear now, completely normal, and anger was welling like a twisted knot inside him.

"Now you are one of us—we can join together in the Acts of Love." Sherry unzipped the back of her dress and let the cloth fall to the floor into a circle around her legs.

Carl's breath caught in his chest at the sight of her body.

She slipped out of her bra and then stood before him, smiling, inviting, and waiting for him to take her into his arms.

It didn't seem possible. After all these weeks, never even a kiss from Sherry, and then all he had to do was go to this house, let them say a few mumbo-jumbo words over him—take him into a small room, drug his mind so that he would believe he was seeing the Devil. It was all insane. But what was more insane was the fact that they believed it. What kind of people could these be? Surely they must know it was one hell of a classic bunko racket. It had to be for some other reason—maybe because these people, like Sherry, needed an excuse to be immoral—to enjoy life—and used this screwed-up way to get around their own prudish restrictions. A nice racket.

"Carl," Sherry murmured. She was lying on the small bed, her arms stretched out for him. "Come, Carl...come to me."

Her breasts were rising and falling rapidly as he moved to her. He drew the full, voluptuous form tightly against his, he kissed the soft fullness of her red lips. A moan issued from her mouth as she squirmed against him. Her body tightened convulsively as he caressed the fullness of her breasts. In the next hour they explored all the forms of love, learning the intimate secrets of one another in the most delightful bed-session Carl had ever experienced.

Later, when they were driving home, he turned to her and asked: "Tell me, how'd you get mixed up with such a...an organization?"

"My father knew about it. My mother knew about it. That's how they happened to meet each other. And since they fell in love—well, they married. As you know, they couldn't do anything like that with anybody outside the organization."

"Oh, don't tell me you really believe that? Surely you're intelligent enough to know it's merely an excuse and —"

"Don't, Carl. You don't know what you're saying. Just wait a few days—just wait. Then come to me—I'll always be waiting for you. I'll always be ready for you," she murmured promisingly.

That was a promise well worth being silent for, he thought. If she wanted to believe all that crap which the 'Organization' offered her, that was all the better for him.

It was some weeks later, when he was in his large office and his secretary came into the room, wiggling her tight little hips in his direction that he learned the truth. She had been on vacation for the last couple of weeks, so it was the first time he had seen her since his membership in tile Satanic Cult. During those weeks he'd explored the bed-sharing exercises with Sherry, and had been completely happy— happier than he'd ever been in his life. It had almost been tempting to suggest they move into the same apartment together—but the only drawback was the fact that he had other women he'd been enjoying—one of whom was his charming little secretary.

Judy romped up to his chair, leaned over and touched his check with her lips. "Hi, boss—how about some overtime?"

He looked at his watch, seeing it was well past six. That surprised him.

But what was more surprising was the strange cold feeling which poured over his nerves.

Sleep with Judy? he thought, looking up into her eyes, letting his gaze examine her bouncy figure. *Sleep with Judy?*

She plopped down onto his lap, sliding her arms around his neck.

Ravish her naked body to his? Smother his lips against her full, voluptuous breasts? Enjoy the wild, furious passion of her over-charged body?

Sleep with Judy?

Ice chilled every nerve in him. He felt cold waves of sickness jab at his stomach.

Sleep with Judy?

"Judy—no. I can't do that. I can't ever do it with you." The words just popped out of his lips, without any thought, without awareness that he was going to say it.

Judy frowned, her face flushed with anger and hurt.

What's wrong?" she moaned.

"I can't do it with you!" he cursed, suddenly realizing what was happening.

And when he realized that, he couldn't believe it.

That drug inspired Devil dream—it couldn't be real, his mind screamed in panic. Yet the very idea of having any relations with anybody other than a cult member suddenly was impossible, sickening, disgusting. It left him completely cold.

But surely it was a trick of his imagination, he thought. It had to be.

He reached for Judy, his arms circling her body, his lips moving closer to hers. Then suddenly he pushed her away, smiled embarrassedly and said:

"I'm sorry—you don't know...but...well, to be truthful—I'm engaged to be married. It wouldn't be right to Sherry."

Judy's face suddenly froze. Her eves became hardened

171

and then after a moment, she brightened, saving: "Well, damn it all, and I thought I had the inside track!"

He considered, he could tell Judy about the cult, and everything would be all tight. He could get all his old girl friends into the Cult, and they would be all his—there was no question about that.

Then he re-considered. Sherry and her lovely body that writhed so delightfully against his. A woman that knew all there was to know about the arts of sensual love was surely more than enough to keep him happy and content for a long while. If not, there were many other members of the cult, some actually quite attractive—though not anywhere as lovely and hot as Sherry..

What did he need another woman for when he had his lovely Sherry?

Laughing, Carl made up his mind: maybe he would move into an apartment with Sherry. Even if it meant marriage. At least he would know how he stood with her. And he could see to it that she never went to the club meetings without him—and therefore could never step out on him.

Hell, he thought, later, as he was getting into his car, *maybe things were better than he had ever thought imagined.*

He had money, charm and looks and one of the best women in the world. What else could he want?

And they would be together for a very long time!

ɞFITTE THE TWENTY-SIXTHଔ

Talk about people! Plotting and planning and betraying. Even in passion they can be deceptive and dangerous. But why oh why did this have to happen to such...

*THREE LOVELY PEOPLE*ଔ

"Do it tonight," Pat Wells whispered, pressing her naked body closer to his,

Her breast trembled under his touch, as it sought closer, more violent contact, it was rising and falling in rhythm with her heavy breath.

"Tonight," she murmured huskily, biting his ear lobe with her lips. The inner softness of their silken surface was moist.

Ben felt her body twist under him, and the suggestive movement sent aching excitement through his impatient, burning nerves.

Hungrily he sought the velvety fullness of her mouth with his.

She stiffened slightly.

"Tonight?" her voice rasped, hardly above a whisper. "It'll happen tonight, then?"

He sighed, and nodded.

She clawed him viciously to her, grinding her open mouth up onto his, convulsively writhing her whole body.

They had known each other for years, ever since he and her husband had started mining their claim.

And in the last few months they had found a mutual de-

173

sire, a terrible affection for each other. But not until this morning, with her husband up at the mine, had they ever found the opportunity for the consummation of their passions.

Now there was plenty of time, all day; hours to playfully excite each other's bodies, passionately exploit the sexual urgency that had been building up in them for so long.

And then, later that evening...

He pushed those ugly thoughts from his mind, and concentrated on the exciting softness of her trembling form under him.

Tonight was far away...

* * * * * * *

Pat felt a sickness inside her, as Ben made his animal, rough kind of love to her.

It revolted her so completely that her body trembled violently to his every caress.

If he only knew...

Somehow she hoped she would be able to force herself to stand his terrible clawing, rubbing, kissing, and bodily contact for all these horrible hours ahead of them.

For money she had to stand it! So much depended on that.

Then afterwards, when he had killed her husband, she'd get even...a few poisonous pills, a bullet in the back, or a knife in the gut—it would be easy!

And the law would say she was justified.

After all, hadn't he killed her husband in cold blood?

Then all the money would be hers. All that lovely...

* * * * * * *

The dark, shadowy form moved in the blackness of the hall. Not a sound followed his footsteps.

Sweat was like a thick coating on his skin. He felt sick inside. He knew his hands were shaking.

But he had no choice...it was now or never! That much he did know.

174

FLUFF, BY CHARLES NUETZEL

He moved carefully, step by step, toward the darkened room at the end of the hall.

The last few months had been like a horrible dream. Watching, and seeing; knowing what was going on—and not being able to do anything about it

He was almost there...

Just a few more steps.

The door was open, and he moved quietly forward.

Looking into the room, he could just barely make out the two forms moving on the bed in the corner.

It was just as he had imagined it.

In one swift movement he pointed the pistol in his hand toward the two naked bodies.

It made him sick.

Joe Wells pulled the trigger over and over, until his wife Pat, and his partner Ben, stopped their agonized twitching.

Then he crumpled to the floor, sobbing and whimpering.

Why had she done it? Why?

಄FITTE THE TWENTY-SEVENTH಄

Some men have seductive tricks up their sleeves, or hidden in the backs of their tongues, which they'll use only in moments of desperation. Now this fellow could sure be a tricky one. He'd even say, like many a likely lad, these magic words to get his hands on a lovely lady…

YOU CAN'T TAKE IT WITH YOU಄

You can't take it with you when you're gone was Forrest Raymore's theme song, if you could call it a song. But he hummed that tune over and over, to every girl he met.

"Honey, what are you saving it for?" he'd smile, reaching eagerly toward her sacred jewels. "You can't take it with you when you're gone...so come on, let's have a ball!"

Usually it worked.

That is to say, he managed to get the gifts of valued love from every maiden he came in contact with. After all, there was a lot of truth in what he said.

And they saw the wisdom in it.

But there are always those who just don't listen to reason, and it was only natural that he would run into one of these young ladies at one time or another.

As it turned out, it came sooner than he would have wished. But then, anytime would have been too soon for him.

She was a lovely creature. Tiny, delightful, laughing, warm, innocent, child-like, and a prude!

"Honey, what are you saving it for?" he chided, reaching

176

eagerly toward those tiny knots of silk on her chest.

She stiffened. Her eyes turned icy blue. Her jaw set. Her hands clinched into hard balls.

"Don't you dare!" she cried in alarm.

"You can't take it with you when you're gone!" he explained, ignoring her lack of response and continued his anxious attempts to caress those curving double scoops of cream.

She squirmed away from him.

"How dare you!" her lips snapped like rigid steel.

"Now baby, Ruthie, honey, don't be childish!" he scolded, smiling fatherly. "After all, I'm only normal and you're such a luscious darling...what did you expect?"

"Not what you think!" she announced with determination. "What do you take me for?"

"A delightful little lady. Warm. Affectionate. Passionate. Honest. And..." He wondered if he should say the thought which had just occurred to him. After all, it wasn't the truth, and he hated to lie. But then it was just petty larceny in a *way*. "And...well, to tell the truth, I love you!"

Her face lighted. She smiled excitedly. Happy tears ran down her cheeks.

"Oh, darling, then that's different!" she yelled with excitement, falling in his arms

ഐFITTE THE TWENTY-EIGHTHᏏ

Another look at the way people get ahead in Hollywood. Or, rather, how one woman managed to make ends meet in such a way that it satisfied her immediate needs without being forced onto…

*THE CASTING COUCH*Ꮟ

Ruth James looked longingly at the man as he entered the coffee shop, and almost wished that she could be like other girls willing to put out to a man. She knew him, instantly. He was very popular with a lot of the women at Sherman Agency. And he had a wild reputation. And she instantly found herself staring at him. Somebody like Dave Carson was worth the price it would cost.

Plus he had helped many women in their careers. But mostly into a bedroom for a one-night stand.

She sighed and took a sip of her coffee, trying to look away from the dark and handsome playboy. The only kind of tumble that he would give a girl was in the rack, and Ruth wasn't the type to give out to *any* man, first date, or last, unless it ended in marriage.

Yet, she thought, this was one man she could find herself giving in to, *if there ever was one.*

The trouble with her was that she'd never gotten rid of her small town ideas. Here she was, twenty-three, in Hollywood, trying to scrape together some kind of existence, while at the same time wanting to break into show business. Most girls her age had had many men, and knew pretty much

178

the score.

And what was Ruth James? she asked herself, bitterly. A young girl, almost as innocent as the day she was born, with bills up to her ears, and not one step closer to Hollywood stardom than she was when she'd left her home in New Mexico. What was going to be the turning point?

"Hello, miss," a low, man's voice interrupted her thoughts.

Ruth looked up, startled. For a moment she was dazed and confused. And while she was taking in the handsome features of Dave Carson, who was standing there looking down at her, she felt a crimson flush moving up her face.

"Oh...hello!" she managed to gulp out.

"I was wondering if I could share your table."

"What?" she cried, in alarm.

He stared at her for a moment and then smiled. "Well, I guess it *was* a little awkward, but I noticed you looking at me, and you *are* quite an attractive young woman—and well, to be honest, I wondered if you would be interested in getting acquainted."

That was blunt, confident and amazingly brazen of the man. Only a rich, successful playboy would be so casually aggressive.

Yet it was thrilling the way he simply took command of the situation, totally unconcerned as to the possibility that she would instantly reject his blunt advance. She was a total stranger sparks were flying in every direction between them.

It took Ruth several seconds to control the fluttering at the pit of her stomach, but finally she managed to quiet it enough to say in a low whisper: "I don't know you. And, well, I'm not the kind of girl that...well, flirts with strange men and..."

"Of course you aren't!" he bellowed, "That's why I was interested."

That sure was a swift shift in gears, without some much of a breath of hesitation. What skill and, damn it, charm.

She was fascinated, despite herself.

He sat down before she could stop him.

"How could you know?"

He laughed, lightly. "How do I know the sky is blue?

179

After seeing it a couple of times you accept the fact. I can tell a lot about a woman."

She looked down at her coffee cup, nervously. "I don't even know you!"

"Come on, now Miss James. I think you know who I am."

She looked up, startled that he knew her name. "How——"

"I know all the pretty women's names. That's my business."

"Oh?"

"Well, I'll be honest with you." He became suddenly serious. "As you surely must know, I work for *Templeton Productions,* and I've seen you around the casting office. Well, with a little checking it wasn't hard to find your name."

"I just came from an interview from there."

"I know. I actually followed you!"

"You're kidding!"

"I'm quite serious." He paused for a moment and then looked directly into her eyes. "You have a charm about you, something fresh, that could be used...I mean, that with a proper promotional action behind you, it would be possible to arrange a rather interesting career."

"What kind of line is that?" Ruth snapped, suddenly angry, finding that she could see right through his little seduction-scheme. "I'm not a child, *Mr. Carson!"*

If her statement was a surprise to him, or moved him, he didn't give any outward signs. "No, Miss James, I'm quite serious!"

For a long moment she stared at him, almost coldly. She considered her options. She could play shocked, insulted, flattered or be just down right brazenly businesslike about it, as if she took him seriously. It took only a moment to decide. She said in an evenly controlled voice: "Just what kind of *deal* are you offering?"

He didn't answer her for a moment, and then he seemed to make up his mind. "Okay, tell you what. You come to my apartment tonight and——"

She stood abruptly, declaring:

"That's what I thought!"

"No! *Wait!"* he cried, reaching out a hand and placing it

on her arm. The contact was strangely exciting. "I'm serious!"

"I just best you are!" she cried back, angrily, brushing his hand off her arm, and trying hard to keep the emotion from her voice and face. The fiery desire was raging through her.

"There's a party. Believe me. About ten couples. I really don't have any particular woman for the evening—and you'll be perfectly safe!"

The sound of his voice convinced her that he was telling the truth. She relaxed and sat down. "In that case, I guess I should be flattered!"

"Not at all. You're quite an attractive woman—I'm the one flattered—if you come!"

If this was a line, he was a master of it. She willingly took his address and everything needed to meet him later. Then she smiled as he walked away a little while after that.

How interesting, she thought, amazed herself, *he's really rather nice.*

* * * * * * *

Dave Carson grinned as he returned to his office. Walking into the casting director's room he exclaimed:

"Well, I think you're about to lose a bet!"

The elder man frowned and glared at Dave. "You mean I was wrong about her?"

"Not that—just that I've gotten to first base! That's all. She's coming to the party tonight."

"I think you're wasting your time, Dave!"

"Why? She's attractive. Beautiful. Small town and a little old fashioned; but with a line, I bet I'll have her in bed within a week!"

"Why are you so interested? After all, you could have any woman you wanted."

"That's not it really. The conversation we had was simply on the basis that Ruth James wasn't suited for any work in our office because she wasn't willing to put out. I stated that with that kind of figure, and those intelligent eyes, a hard working Hollywood con-man could make the scene

181

with her. You claimed that it was impossible. So—I'm going to prove you wrong!"

"But what's the point?"

"Simple. We can always use a girl like her on the line. If she can act at all, it would bring in a few bills. And, there is the other point: a girl, willing to put out to one man will be willing to put out to others—the best way to keep producers happy!"

"I know the rules."

"So—I'll break her in!" Dave exclaimed, sure of himself. "Then we sign her to a contract, sending her around for interviews—producers give her a line, offer her a small part, take her to bed, and if she is worth it, they'll really give her the part!" He laughed and then added: "Simple !"

* * * * * * *

"Dave Carson?" Ruth's roommate cried, excitedly. "To a party?"

"Well, that's just as far as it is going to go!" Ruth snapped, pulling her bra around the full, firm shape of her breasts. She looked at herself in the mirror. She had a good, seductive figure. Maybe if she played her cards right she might be able to wiggle a contract out of Carson.

That would take care of her end of the rent. And she *did* need money! The landlady had stopped her in the hallway on her way up to the room. Everybody wanted money!

But she'd be damned if she'd let Dave Carson seduce her for the chance of a contract! That was one thing that Ruth James just wouldn't do.

* * * * * * *

The party was noisy and wild. A couple was playing the piano and two other people standing around, listening. Drinks were flowing free. The swank apartment was filled with mingling people moving from one group to another. Must of it was "working the room!"

"I thought you said they'd be about a dozen couples," Ruth whispered, staring into the dark eyes of Dave Carson.

182

He smiled and took a sip of his highball. "Invite a dozen and you will get five dozen. Hollywood party crashers! It happens every time! And a lot of business is closed out in such events, or just merely opened up!"

Ruth looked at the man and after nervously biting her lower lip, she asked: "You really think that there is a chance that I'll get a contract?"

Carson looked seriously back at her. "You have a chance—like any attractive woman. If you can act, and make people, *important people*, like you, there's no reason why you can't go a long way. Look at this room! Filled with important contacts!"

He reached out and caressed her white shoulder, gazing momentarily down toward the revealing neck-line. "You really *are* a beautiful woman. What brought you to Hollywood?"

"Same old story. Young small town girl wants to get into movies," she stated, emotionlessly.

He nodded, sure of himself. "Come along with me!" he told her, taking her hand in his and pulling her along.

She followed, feeling a light grinding warning catch in her stomach. He had fed her with several strong drinks, and she was afraid of what she might do.

He led her though the living room, past all the people, and then down a hall and into a small bedroom. Before she could do anything to stop him, he had closed the door behind her.

"You said you wouldn't try anything!" she warned, moving away from him, fear fluttering through her, ice moving down her spine.

"What's with you? You aren't afraid?" he asked, smiling. "I won't do anything you don't want me to do. I just wanted to be alone with you!"

She relaxed for a second, and in that instant he stepped forward and pulled her into his arms. She tensed. Freezing.

His lips were very close to hers and she could feel a reaction moving down her spine, cutting away the ice and changing it into a warmth she hadn't felt for over a year. The strong, powerful urge of desire.

"No!" she managed to choke a split moment before their

lips met.

Then she felt herself giving in. The feel of his body next to hers was more exciting that she could have though it would be. His lips pressed to hers and then gently parted.

To her horror she felt her own mouth opening. Then all hell broke loose through her body. Fire burned. Electric sparks jumped from nerve to heated nerve. Her face flushed and she became weak in his arms, then felt herself tensing against his body.

Oh, what was she letting herself do? her mind screamed in terror. His hand began to caress her. Fire ached through her again, overwhelming her resistance. Then he lifted her up in his arms and started carrying her to bed.

That's when the ice returned. Ice of fear. Ice of self disgust. Ice of determination.

"No!" she said, struggling.

He kept hold of her, but paused.

"No!" she repeated, firmly, looking into his eyes.

He started at her, shock showing in his face. "You kidding?"

"No!"

Slowly he led her down on her feet. "You're a little fool!" he snapped, nastily. "This was your big chance. If you'd proven yourself worthy—there'd have been a contract for you!"

Her face went white and furry sparked in her eyes. Then without even realizing what she was doing, her hand slapped forcefully across his face.

She was rushing out of the room, leaving him standing there numbed.

Ruth got outside before the anger simmered down. For a long time she stood on the front porch, thinking. Then she started walking.

The night air was cooling and the desperate fire of anger, with its strong mixture of passionate desire, slowly began to loose some of its strength.

She realized that she should go back.

Back to the apartment. It had taken a long time for her to get even this far in Hollywood. Months. The rent was due, she owed money to the Gas, Electric and Water companies.

She owed money to her roommate. She couldn't leave town, even if she wanted to. And the only out was to go get a job and that would be the end of any quick chances to a quick climb up in the movies.

He had offered a contract. That would mean a little money—if he was telling the truth. And Dave Carson was one hell of a man. She realized that if she'd met him in her home town, and gone out with him long enough, they might have ended in bed. She was strongly attracted to him.

The only thing this was Hollywood. And a girl who gave out to casting directors, producers, directors, or just playboys with "pull," either got the lay-job and thrown aside, or *really* got the contracts.

She had seen a lot of important people in the house, at Carson's party. She had seen people who, if she got to know them, could do her a lot of good.

If she got to know them...

That thought drifted off. *But she wouldn't get to know them.*

She didn't have any assurance that Dave Carson was telling the truth about giving her a contract. But if he was— then all her problems would be over—for the while. And then she'd have a chance to meet some of the other, powerful people.

Suddenly she paused, startled at the thought which had just whipped through her mind.

She was twenty-two, and an adult, and why not?

Morality?

Not really. Because she knew that the real law of morality was simply that two adults could do anything they wanted together, as long as they weren't hurting anybody else but themselves—and knew exactly what they were doing. Morality was a personal thing. If you did something and then, later, couldn't live without guilt, then that was immoral.

It was also immoral to owe people money. And, to her, it would be immoral for her to get a job—outside of show-business—because that would defeat her whole purpose of coming to Hollywood.

There came a time in everybody's life when they had to face up to reality of Hollywood was that you had to please to get ahead. You had to make friends and contacts. She had learned *that* much since she'd come here.

Sudden fear shot through her. *Maybe it was already too late.* She stopped walking, turned and started back to the house. When she got there, she walked in, looked through the living room. It took her only a few moments to spot Carson. He was talking to a tall, gray-haired man, who she had been introduced as a powerful producer.

She walked up to them and grabbed hold of his arm. "Dave, I have something important to tell you!"

He looked toward her, anger flared in his face, "What do you want!"

"Just come with me!"

"Leave me alone!" he snapped.

The producer cut in, his voice amused: "If I were you, I'd listen to her!"

"But this is the one I was telling you—"

The producer smiled and said: "Would you be interested in talking to me, young lady?"

She stared at the man, startled. This changed things completely. He wasn't her type. He wasn't the kind of man that she could find herself interested in, in the least.

Dave broke in, quickly:

"I think I have something to talk to *you* about!" he said, taking Ruth's arm and pulling on it.

She smiled at the producer. "It would be—well, you can see—some other time?"

He nodded, delighted.

Dave Carson moved her through the room and then stopped at the hallway, his face showing real surprise. "He's really interested in you. If you played the cards right..."

Suddenly she realized that she didn't have to sleep with Carson. He was eager to sign her up, because of the producer. A feeling of disappointment moved through her, as she looked at the tall handsome man. And all of a sudden she realized the truth. She'd sleep with him—regardless! That startled her, but not enough to keep her from taking hold of the man's hand and leading him down the hall. He followed, numbly.

A moment later she was closing the door behind them.

186

"You wanted me to be friendly. So..." she announced, reaching behind her and unzipping her dress. It fell to the floor around her legs. She didn't pause, but unclasp the bra and slid it off. Her breasts burst outwards and she eagerly removed her pink panties.

Standing before him she said: "I guess this doesn't really have anything to do with the contract we'll be signing tomorrow, does it?"

He stared blankly at her for a moment and then laughed.

"I guess not," he agreed, beginning to get undressed.

✍FITTE THE TWENTY-NINTH✍

Talk about fluff; well it's about time we saw a bit of sci-fi hot air flying around in the outer limits of our universe. Now I promise you, this may not be more than fluff, with the "once upon a time" opening. Just remember: I never promised more than that. But we all need at least one...

KEEPER OF THE STARS✍

Once upon a time there was a man who could never find the girl of his dreams.

That is to say, the girl of his dreams would have to be one with unlimited powers in the matters of sexual relations.

Oh, it can't be said that he never was satisfied in matters of love, but it would take a very heavy schedule to fulfill his large hunger. Not only in numbers, but in size, shape and style.

One moment he was wanting large-breasted, narrow-hipped women; the next it would be ping-pong-size chest development. Or maybe large treasures and wide hips.

But never could he be completely happy with only one woman.

And it can honestly be said that he raped the universe in his search for the one and only delight of his dreams. A girl that could really come out with the goods, with such complete and loving care that he would never again have to have another female.

And then finally in his search he began to hear rumors about a kingdom ruled by a Queen, with such sexual habits that not one man had ever been able to keep up with her.

But, at first, he could not find out exactly where this world, or worlds, which she ruled was.

He looked on every star chart of the explored universe, and even studied old maps which were drawn in electric pencil, or charcoal, and even in old-fashioned lead pencil. But there was no reference of the Queen of his desires.

Then, one day a friend of his happened to meet him on the street, and invited him up to his apartment for a drink.

"Jab, my old friend," he said happily, patting the man on the back, "Nothing I'd love better."

"For one like you, Annow, a drink is hardly fitting."

Arm in arm they went to the man's living quarters, a seven room place which was push button controlled— modern and expensive even for their times.

"What'll you have?" Jab asked, as they seated themselves on a large wide sofa.

"A Galactic Star!" Annow said, his mouth watering at the very thought of that expensive drink.

"You shall have it! And I too!" the bearded Jab cried, pressing a button at the side of the couch. A robot appeared and took their orders. Two seconds later he produced the drinks out of thin air.

Sipping his "punch" Annow delighted in the soothing electric excitement, as it worked through his body. He looked at his tall, dark-haired friend. "How long has it been...since we saw each other last?"

Jab smiled and leaned back, thinking hard. "Well over five years...and what wonderful years they have been..."

"You look as if they involved a woman...if you are the same Jab I used to know."

"Woman? Woman? Ha! That is one hell of a universal laugh." He grew serious for a moment, then leaned forward, peering at his friend intently. "Would you like to hear a story that will really burn your ears? About the *Keeper of the Stars*?"

"Sounds interesting!"

"Well, now...don't laugh, and don't think I'm just day dreaming...or space dreaming for that matter. This is true, though unbelievable."

189

"I was out in space, beyond the reaches of space itself; out in the infinity that spans the galaxy. Out there is the kingdom of two solar systems, one natural, the other artificial, which is ruled by a Queen called *The Keeper of the Stars*!"

Annow stood upright, shocked and jolted. He couldn't believe his ears. After all these years of searching...here was his old friend who had discovered the dream woman of his life!

"It can't be true...the Queen that glories of such sexual excitement that no man has ever satisfied her?" he cried, standing eagerly, and even trembling a little.

Surprise showed on Jab's long features. "How did you know?"

"Oh, friend of friends...how do I know?" he exclaimed in mocked horror.

Then he told him of his search, ending with: "But how did you discover the place?"

"I was lost in space with a faulty space-drive. I just ended up there."

"Can you take me to the kingdom?" Annow questioned anxiously.

"Yes...but if what you are planning is what I think consider carefully before you enter upon the journey for there are barbs along the way!"

"I fear not!" he said stoutly.

"There is a test that you must pass before attaining the glory of the Queen's body!" his friend warned. "I but tried, and gave up..."

That surprised him to almost a standstill. He felt a chill run through him, for Jab was one of the few men of reputation that he could even come near admiring.

But he shook himself, and bravely stated, "I fear not!"

And so it was that he was directed to the Kingdom, that claimed to be the *Keeper of the Stars*; and once there he could well understand the reason for the name. The lens of the Galaxy stretched across the night sky like a gigantic island in space. Truly, if anything could be called keeper, it would be this small two-solar system kingdom.

He landed on the capital planet, where the Queen lived,

190

and where the tests were held for the one night stand with her. For it was said that one night with her satisfied a man's desires for a woman for the rest of his life. For the Queen was most exhausting, and most perfect in the art of making love.

No man had satisfied her.

"You wish to enter the test?" the officer said staring at him as if he were insane.

He nodded eagerly.

"You understand that the tests are very difficult to pass...but once passed you win the glory of attaining the bed of the Queen."

He signed the necessary papers. The man pressed a button, and instantly he was transported through space to a small bed chamber, where the most beautiful woman he had ever seen lay naked on a bed.

Such mountains of breasts. Such large, wide, desirable hips. Such red lips.

Never had he seen such a woman.

He walked over to her and took that beautiful body to his.

Her hips were pure vibrating fire, burning with such heat that he became weak and helpless. Her teeth bruised and cut him wherever they touched.

But as violent as she was, he matched it with his own violence.

He found himself lying on another bed. Larger and softer. A different woman was naked next to him.

She smiled.

Stars exploded in him. Emotions welled that had never been sparked before. Love came like a gigantic wave of electric fire.

She was it.

The best, most voluptuous, desirable entity he had ever seen.

And they didn't wait...

They took each other.

Later, much later, she stirred and demanded his gift of love again.

And it started once more. The two greatest lovers in the

universe explored each other, and exploited the emotions and passions and loves, and never stopped to rest, until exhaustion took control.

And he knew that at last he had found the one for him; and knew she felt the same way as he did.

The Queen of the *Keeper of the Stars* looked down at her lover and sighed. "You...you were wonderful..." she said helplessly, then collapsed exhausted.

He had bettered the best. He was happy. Fantastically happy.

So once upon a time, there was a man who found his loving mate...and.

Like they say in all story books...

They loved happily ever after!

&FITTE THE LAST&

*And if that doesn't do the trick, [and it should have with its
"happily ever after" then this addition is offered up for a bit
of final fluff: a bit of seductive advice which was offered up
as an article, of sorts. Consider this a sound warning that the
following is, hopefully,*

ENOUGH, BUT NOT TOO MUCH&

Any good Don knows that a few drinks now and then
aren't so bad, as long as you know when you've had
enough—but, not too much!

A much better idea—while on the job (seduction, to the
squares)—is not to drink at all!

The reason should be obvious enough, but just in case a
few readers—boozers, that is—don't get the picture, try pic-
turing this scene:

You've just walked into the party. A real wild affair
with women all over the place. Needless to say these girls
know the ropes and the scores—they're keeping track of
each other, so that one won't get ahead of the game. Never
have you seen such a group of almost—but, sadly, not
quite—exposed breast-advertisements. One glance at any of
these dipping breast-lines and there is no doubt in your mind
that given enough time—a few minutes and a few lines—that
any one of these full bloomed twins will burst forward, exposing all.

Since that is your mission in life—exposing as many
"alls" as possible—you quickly make it a point to grace-

193

fully—that means smoothly—move over to makeshift bar in the corner of the room where several half empty—or half full, depending on how you look at it—liquor bottles are sitting invitingly ready for the eager young drunk—man, or woman—to dip into their spiritual dimension of fantasy.

Well, as it so many times has happened in the past, you have already had a couple of cocktails—martinis (six gin to one dry vermouth—along with six olives to absorb the effects)—before dinner and then a couple at a friend's place.

Realizing the already happy-glow, which is trying to make a numb band around your head, is just at the very border of getting out of control, you look for gin.

No sooner have you noticed a bottle than you see that it is empty.

That's fine! You nod foolishly to yourself, not aware of the pretty blonde girl in the dipping blue dress who has just slid up to you.

Well, what the hell? you figure, knowing that you will look pretty square without a drink in your hands—and that could be dangerous in a group like this. Taking the half-full bottle of rum, you boldly drop a couple of half-melted ice cubes into a water glass, and then, having now noticed the girl, you overshoot your wad!

What lovely curves, your eyes are screaming in delight, as they make a complete sweep of her sensual topography and then gain contact with her widely innocent, blue ones. She smiles and just about this time you are pouring the liquor into the glass. Naturally it almost over-flows.

The expression of shock in her lovely eyes calls to your attention what has been happening to that water glass in your hands. You look and feel a tight knot of embarrassment flood through you—but, bravely you hold it down.

Laughingly, you gaily add a little soda water and a dash of bitters and twist of lemon to what looks like something around six jiggers of pure 97 Proof Jamaican Rum. "Always fix myself a Jamaican Spice!" you explain quickly, coming up with the greatest come-back since Frank Sinatra zoomed into fame a few years ago. "Like one?"

By this time the amazement is open admiration. Her perfectly sexual, full-bodied, red and silky looking, lips moving

194

open for a long moment—while you watch the delightful nervous jerk of her delicate tongue—and then she finally manages to overcome her shock by choking out, "You mean that you drink that kind of drink all the time?"

Now you've done it.

Well, what the hell, you exclaim silently, examining her more pointedly lovely features again, all for the cause and all rot-gut!

And down the hatch goes this new creation called Jamaican Spice.

It hits your stomach. Quivers. Shakes. Explodes to fire and then bounces up to your head like a snapping electric charge—what ever that is, and by this time you couldn't care less.

You look at all three of her, who are trying to divide into six and then attempting to combine back into one—she doesn't seem to want to make up her mind whether to be one or six—and you're in no condition to make it up for her.

After the first numbing jolt you suddenly don't feel so bad, especially since the little sex-machine has finally decided on becoming two—and has settled solidly at that number.

"Well, girls!" you say, attempting to take hold of each with a different arm, realizing that it will really make a good impression on the others to see you leave with two twin sisters, one on each arm. "Let's go!"

She's all the time trying to find the other girl and the slow, burning fury in her eyes is about to erupt into an explosive volcano. Naturally you don't notice.

Then when you are just about to pull her apart at the seams in your attempt at getting the two girls separated, she blows-up!

Into a million pieces.

One moment she is there and the next she is gone.

You hardly notice her angry face and figure, as it races across the room away from you, because suddenly the floor is your center of interest—then you're making love to it (and that is pure heaven—in fact, dream-time).

So, you see, what can start out to be a great evening with a girl who is not only just about the most sexy thing you ever did see but who is ready willing and anxious, will end up with you on the floor, stoned to the gills because you've had more than enough—and much too much!

The way to avoid such a situation is not to have anything before coming to the party—or, at least, nothing too strong. Maybe one mild drink will be all right, but be sure that you have coated your stomach with something greasy before and after—this will take care of the over-boozing effects of the grab-what-you-can at the party.

So, taking that scene over for a slight rewrite so that we can we can see the dramatic difference:

Realizing that you don't want to feel your drinks too much you have taken the above advice and are ready to conquer the world—or the women might be a better phrase.

You quickly make it a point to gracefully move over to the makeshift bar in the corner of the room where several half-empty liquor bottles are sitting invitingly reach for any eager young Don—or Jean—to dip into their spiritual dimension of fantasy.

You are well aware that anything you might have will be all right, since the before dinner drink was sandwiched in between olive oil and a greasy meal, and so you grab the first bottle there is.

A very good scotch. Taking a water glass you plunk a couple of ice cubes into it and then begin pouring the scotch over them.

Up until now you haven't noticed the beautiful redhead—naturally this is a different time and a different party and a different girl—who has just slipped up next to you. The feel of her silky firm thigh as it presses against your's brings your attention to her bulging double scoop of mountainous breasts which are having the bottle-of-the-bulge with the Kelly green dress which almost doesn't hide the delightfully pink centers of her more pointed spots of interest.

Your stomach does a turn.

What a woman. Her eyes are pure fire. Her lips are already half parted and the way she moistens them there is no doubt in our mind that given the chance—that is, if you were alone in the world with her—she would strip off the restraining dress and be more than happy to make with the jazz right

196

then.

You stomach is so excited with nervous anxiety that you quickly gulp the scotch. It hits like an acid bomb. It explodes like an atomic bomb, blowing your brains clear out of your skull.

Peeling yourself off the ceiling you glibly take hold of her arm and you both start across the room.

That's when it hits you.

You stomach is churning wildly. You suddenly realize—too late—that what ever you had for dinner—by this time you couldn't remember your mother's name, let along what you had for dinner—just didn't mix good with scotch.

Well, you can't win all the time.

Politely knocking the redhead down and almost stepping on her, you quickly—that means running at top speed—start heading in the direction of another—more private—room where you will possibly get away with being violently ill.

Naturally, from that moment on, the evening is ruined for you.

As it was said at the beginning, any good Don knows that a few drinks now and then aren't so bad, as long as you know when you've had enough—but, not too much!

Well, that applies to food, too—especially greasy food.

But then, any Don foolish enough to over-do the drinking part of the evening is liable to over do anything...

Which goes to prove—if nothing else—that one must know when to quit, they must learn moderation, they must learn to never over do anything.

In other words: have enough—but, not too much!

Which is somewhat of an ideal closer for this collection of outright Fluff!

∞CREDITS∝

"Don't Cry Tonight" was published in 1962 in *Las Vegas Showgirl.*

"Party Business" was published in 1962 in *Las Vegas Showgirl.*

"The Stand-In" was published in 1962 in *Las Vegas Showgirl.*

"A Reputation at Stake" was published in 1962 in *Las Vegas Showgirl.*

"Couch Interview" was published in 1962 in *Las Vegas Showgirl.*

"A Pocket Full of Pleasure" was published in 1963 in *Gusto.*

"In Defense of Prostitution" was published in 1963 in *Gusto.*

"Bribery in Flesh" was published in 1960 in *Candid.*

"Picked Up to Be Raped" was published in 1960 in *Black Silk Stockings.*

"Cheater Wife" was published in 1960 in *Hollywood Playgirls.*

"Blackmail Reversed" was published in 1961 in *Baby Doll.*

"Hot Day in the Country" was published in 1960 in *King.*

"Suddenly Lust Summer" was published in 1960 in *Sextet.*

"The Passionate Pilgrim" was published in 1961 in *Torch.*

"Nude on a Lonely Beach" was published in 1961 in *Torch.*

"Birth of a Call Girl" was published in 1960 in *Candid.*

"Big Dave's Girls" was published in 1960 in *Mr. Cool.*

"Say Rum, Chum" was published in 1963 in *Jigger.*

"The 21st Step" was published in 1962 in *Kick.*

"Rock 'n' Roll Sweetheart" was published in 1962 in *Strip.*

"The Sizzle Girl" was published in 1962 in *Hippy.*

"She's Something Like a Dame" was published in 1963 in *Red Garter.*

"The Cat and the Canary" was published in 1963 in *Red*

Garter.

"To Hustle a Hustler" was published in 1963 in *Red Garter.*

"Satan's Mistress" was published in 1963 in *Tomcat.*

"Three Lonely People" was published in 1963 in *Gusto.*

"You Can't Take It with You" was published in 1962 in *Nympho.*

"The Casting Couch" was published in 1963 in *Jigger.*

"The Keeper of the Stars" was published in 1960 in *Mr. Cool.*

"Enough, but Not Too Much" was published in the 1960s in *Captivate.*

ଈ୬ABOUT THE AUTHORଈ୬

Charles Nuetzel was born in San Francisco in 1934, and writes:

"As long as I can remember I wanted to be a writer. It was a dream I never thought would materialize. But with the help of Forrest J Ackerman, who became my agent, I managed to finally make it into print.

"I was lucky enough not only in selling my work to publishers but also ending up packaging books for some of them, and finally becoming a 'publisher' much like those who had bought my first novels. From there it as a simple leap to editing not only a science-fiction anthology, but also a line of SF books for Powell Sci-Fi back in the 1960s. Throughout these active professional years I had the chance to design some covers and do graphic cover layouts for pocket books & magazines."

Much of his work in covers and graphics are a result of having had a father who was a professional commercial artist, and who did a number of covers for sci-fi magazines in the 1950s and later for pocket books—even for some of Mr. Nuetzel's books.

In retirement he has become involved in swing dancing, a long time lover of Big Band jazz. But more interestingly world travels have taken him (and his wife Brigitte) across the world, to Hawaii, Caribbean, Mexico, Kenya, Egypt, Peru, having a lifelong interest in ancient civilizations. His website is full of thousands of pictures taken during these trips.